SUSAN Cohn

paper bird

paper bird

A Novel of South Africa

Maretha Maartens

Clarion Books
New York

Clarion Books
a Houghton Mifflin Company imprint
215 Park Avenue South, New York, NY 10003
Copyright © 1989 Maretha Maartens
First published in this English
version in Great Britain 1990 by
MACMILLAN CHILDREN'S BOOKS
A division of Macmillan Publishers Limited
London and Basingstoke
Associated companies throughout the world

First published in South Africa by
Tafelberg Publishers Limited
in Afrikaans in 1987 under the title
Die Inkvoël
in English in South Africa in 1989
under the title *The Ink Bird*
Translated by Madeleine van Biljon
All rights reserved

Library of Congress Cataloging-in-Publication Data
Maartens, Maretha.
[Inkvoël.   English]
Paper bird / by Maretha Maartens ; [translated by Madeleine Van Biljon].
p.   cm.
Translation of: Die inkvoël.
Summary: Because he is responsible for keeping his pregnant mother
and brothers and sisters from starving, young Adam travels daily
from his small black South African township to sell newspapers in
the city, until marauding bands of thugs make this work dangerous
and force him to a difficult decision.
ISBN 0-395-56490-5
[1. Blacks — South Africa — Fiction.   2. South Africa — Race
relations — Fiction.]   I. Title.
PZ7.M1115Pap   1991
[Fic] — dc20   90-39675   CIP   AC

BP 10 9 8 7 6 5 4 3 2 1

paper bird

chapter 1

In Phameng, at that time of evening, there was smoke everywhere, because everyone was lighting fires. When so many people lived together, there was a lot of smoke, in many colors: brown and gray and white, depending on the fuel used.

As quietly as possible Adam slipped through the door, but Paul the Pest stuck his foot out so that he couldn't close it. He tried to kick Paul's foot away but couldn't, expecting Mama Dora's loud voice to call him back. Now you must run, Adam! he thought. Run, before the storm breaks loose.

He knew where Edward would be. Edward never helped with the fire-making, not even now when the sun set so early and the cold of night came in the late afternoon. He was forever wandering around in the open veld in front of the hotel, like a heron that had lost its way. Creep up behind him and you'd catch him talking to himself, or to the few head of cattle. Edward knew the names of all the animals, even though they didn't belong to him. Sometimes the cattle moved off to graze in the direction of Bochabela, and then Edward would throw stones, raising a cloud of dust and ash. Or he would kick the tins and pieces of cardboard, making them fly like a flock of wild birds. When Edward kicked, he kicked like someone who wanted to kill. He hated Phameng. And of all the houses in Phameng, he hated Mama Dora's most, especially when Paul the Pest and Sefanya and Mannetjie were at home.

That evening Edward was standing on the other side of the veld, close to the tarred road that ran between Phameng and Opkoms, where the colored people lived. Arms akimbo, he was staring at one of the cows. Adam sighed and started running. Tonight, for sure, his brother was going to bed hungry. "Edward," he called through his cupped hands. "E-hey!"

One of the gaudily painted Jacaranda buses came rumbling up with its load of late-working women. The women got off at the bus stop and he heard them talking as they headed for home. Edward came walking toward Adam, but even from a distance he could see how angry he was. He took no notice of the falling winter darkness. He kept looking back, jerking his shoulders in a cocky way.

"Mama Dora's going to throw us out of that house," said Adam, and if it hadn't been so cold he would have grabbed Edward by the collar. "You'll get us all thrown out."

"I wish she would," Edward replied. Suddenly he

looked taller to Adam, as if he were as tall as Adam was. "I'm waiting for her to do it!"

"You're an idiot," said Adam, getting crosser and crosser. "Are you going to find Ma a house? You and your big mouth!"

"I'd rather live under pieces of corrugated iron than stay in that place any longer," said Edward. "Mama Dora and her awful children act as though . . . as though we're lice — bedbugs who've crawled into her house! Ma pays her, after all! If we take the money Ma pays Mama Dora each month, we could buy our own iron sheets and build . . ."

"Forget it," said Adam. "How can you put Ma under a few pieces of corrugated iron when she . . . looks the way she does now?"

Edward had no answer. He sighed and glanced over his shoulder again. "I was thinking, this evening," he said. "Do you see what that cow looks like, the one they call Horn? I swear she's eaten a plastic bag again — her stomach is all swollen. Ma looks just like that."

"She's not that bad," said Adam defensively.

"She is," said Edward somberly. "The skin over her feet is going to burst open. I've been watching her. Her skin can't last much longer." He picked up a stone and threw it far across the veld. "Like one of those stupid potatoes that burst open as soon as they're cooked."

"Yes," Adam added, shivering at his own thoughts.

3

"When those potatoes burst, all their insides pop out."

"She can't possibly have another baby right now!" said Edward. He kicked furiously at a tin.

"How could Ma have known that Pa would be killed?" asked Adam. "That baby was inside her before Pa died. She just didn't know what would happen."

"When that baby comes," said Edward, *then* you'll hear Mama Dora! I don't know where the child is going to sleep. There's hardly room for us to lie down. You know what it was like the week when Uncle Saul was home from the mine."

Suddenly, Adam remembered the putu that was cooling on the plate. "We can't stand here talking!" he said and his stomach knotted. "I forgot, Edward. We must run if you want any food tonight. Mama Dora says she won't dish up food for you later!"

He set off at a trot toward the house, but Edward deliberately dawdled behind him in the cold, smoky twilight. "It's no use her trying to spite me," he said, spitting to the left of Adam. "I'm just waiting for Mama Dora to say something . . . just *waiting*!"

Something rumbled on the dirt road between the bus stop and the hotel, rattling over the potholes. Looking around, Adam saw, in the last remaining light, the two Casspirs. His body felt cold, as though everything in him had died. The rumble of the Casspirs sounded like war. The huge monsters wobbled towards him, their lights on — yellow eyes in the twilight.

"Come on, Edward," Adam screamed and his legs suddenly moved of their own accord. "Come on! They'll kill us with those rubber bullets!"

Only then did Edward start running.

The first time the Casspirs came, Adam remembered, there were many more. They were full of policemen in blue riot uniforms. All day long there had been trouble in the streets and at the schools. The children had started throwing stones. Then the Casspirs arrived, and a thunderous voice boomed from the bullhorn: "Go back to your homes! Get off the streets!"

Mama Dora was at work, and Ma scurried around trying to get all the children into the house. She looked like a hen collecting her chicks. "Where is Sefanya?" she asked above the noise, over and over again. "Edward . . . Adam . . . Mannetjie — where is Sefanya?"

No one could answer her. Mannetjie, whose real name was Moses, merely shrugged his shoulders and hung out of the window to see what was going on. Evon and Maria screamed so loudly that Adam wanted to block his ears. His sisters looked like sheep in a drought: all sinew and bones, as their bodies became taut with screaming and terror. They looked so hollow and full of holes that he dreamed about it that night.

In his dream they were skeletons with holes where eyes used to be.

"Do be quiet!" Ma scolded, trying to put her hand over their mouths. "We're in the house. Nothing can happen to us here!"

The Casspirs began spitting smoke and rubber bullets. The people in the street screamed and ran. But one of the young girls, Sophia Bojang, who had a clubfoot, was slow and got hurt. Sophia stuttered in school, but when she lay sprawled in the dust, she howled like a dog. One of the men jumped out of the Casspir and picked her up. She kept on wailing while he dusted off her tattered dress and asked loudly if she was all right. But Sophia tore herself loose like a wild animal and hobbled away. The man was angry: he spoke to the young men in the Casspir and kept pointing in Sophia's direction. He was coughing and the smoke made tears run down his cheeks. For a brief moment it seemed as though the big man in the blue uniform was crying about Sophia, the clubfoot.

Someone spoke over the bullhorn, and Maria crept under the table and sat there, quivering like a mouse. Adam wanted to pray, but he was completely confused. The great voice outside sounded like Modimo's. Was that possible? Where was Modimo? Was he in heaven, above the clouds, or in the Casspirs outside?

Later, when the Casspirs trundled toward the school, he told Ma how confused he'd been, how he had not been able to pray. Her face turned gray, the way it had done when Ntate died. "Don't ever speak that way again!" she scolded. "Those were people, ordinary people. Modimo is in the highest heaven. He is always in the highest heaven."

"Why did those things come here?" Magdalene asked. "Ma, why are they here?"

Ma sat thinking for a long time, her hands folded on her big stomach as though it hurt her to think.

"It's because we don't understand each other," she said after a while, and the pain in her stomach showed in her eyes, and in her voice, too.

"Who?" Edward asked, his mouth full of bread. "Who doesn't understand, Ma?" Suddenly, Sefanya burst through the back door. His face was streaked with dust and dried tears, and there was a bloodstain on one shoulder. Ma drew in her breath sharply, seeing Sefanya's face so wild and dark.

"Who, Ma?" Edward asked again. He gazed with wide eyes at Sefanya, but he wanted an answer. Edward always wanted answers.

Ma got up to help Sefanya; the wound on his shoulder was still bleeding.

"Our people, Edward," she said with difficulty. "The people of our country."

From far away, Adam could hear Evon crying. It was worse than the rumbling of the Casspirs. The sound cut into his head like a knife.

Edward stopped in his tracks. "I thought you said you were eating already. Why is she crying?"

"She was quiet when we started," said Adam. He felt as though he were caught between two fires: on the one hand the men in the Casspirs, on the other, Evon's yells. "Her ear is probably aching again," he added wearily as they went into the house.

Evon was standing on Ma's lap, her bare feet pummeling Ma's big stomach. The harder she pummeled, the more wildly she hit out with her hands. Magdalene was hanging on to her dress, and Maria was sitting on the cement floor next to the chair, her eyes tightly closed.

Mama Dora came up with a spoon in her hand. "Evon!" she scolded, trying to push Evon's head to one side. She wanted to pour warmed oil into her ear, but Evon knocked the spoon from her hand and the oil curved through the air.

It travels more slowly than water, Adam thought in fright. Perhaps as slowly as very dirty dishwater will travel. Water like Mama Dora's dishwater. He waited for Mama Dora to start scolding.

But Ma struggled to her feet and seemed not to notice Evon's small hands hitting her in the face. "Leave it, Dora," she called. "I'll try to plug it with a bit of cottonwool and Vicks, later on."

"She's darned naughty," said Mama Dora and took the spoon Magdalene handed to her. "If she was my child, I'd give her a good hiding."

8

"Her ear is very sore," Ma said gently. "Look how swollen it is; it's standing away from her head."

"It's the screaming that does that," said Mama Dora loudly. "This child must learn to listen when a person is speaking. What am I supposed to do when you have to go to Pelonomi Hospital to have the baby, and this child won't listen to anyone? You're too soft with her, *mosadi*, far too soft."

"Perhaps her ear will be better by the time I have to go to Pelonomi," Ma said. "It's a while yet. Go on, Magdalene, help with the plates, *ausi!*"

Suddenly Ma saw Edward. "This evening you don't get anything," she said over Evon's crying. "We waited and waited, Edward, but if you want to spend your time with the cattle, you can't blame Mama Dora if she gives your food to the others. If you won't listen, you'll have to go hungry." She sighed, relenting. "Take your plate, Adam. Your putu is cold."

Adam saw Edward squaring his shoulders and wanted to stop him, but Edward was already speaking. "Mama Dora hardly waited at all! She just wanted to give my food to Mannetjie and the others!"

Edward's words fell like stones on a tin roof. Suddenly there was a deadly silence in the room. Even Evon was quiet now.

At last Mama Dora spoke. "I don't like the child's manner. You must tell me if you're dissatisfied with this house, Edward. I don't like your manner." Then

9

she added softly, as though she needed heavenly help with such an impossible child: "Modimo!"

Mama Dora's voice silenced everyone, even Edward. He looked to the left and to the right, and when he spoke again, Adam knew that he'd been put in his place for a while.

"I didn't . . . mean to come late, Mama Dora. There was a cow that had eaten a plastic bag and . . ."

"You're not on Dr. Marx's farm any longer," Mama Dora interrupted him, wagging a finger. "The people here don't like children wandering among the cattle. The cows might lose their milk. Cattle aren't things for children to play with. I wonder why that doctor ever allowed you to wander among his cattle like that."

"Ntate had his own cattle, Mama Dora," Maria piped up suddenly from the floor. "Flower and Yellow and Sucker."

Mama Dora sniffed loudly and went outside.

"Sugar!" exclaimed Mama Dora's Moses with a loud laugh. "What a stupid name!"

"Sucker, man!" said Edward, suddenly swinging round as though he wanted to attack Moses. "Because she always drank so greedily from the bottle. She was a pet calf."

"It must've been nice on the farm," said Moses sarcastically. "You probably lay down under the cow's udder and squirted the milk straight into your mouth."

Adam squirmed. "It *was* nice," he said, before

Edward could speak. "There was a dam where we could swim and we had a choir at the farm school. We held choir festivals and . . ."

"You probably sang 'Brother Jacob,' " Paul the Pest said suddenly. He opened his mouth wide and started singing:

> "Bona sekolo, bona sekolo,
> Tlong sekolong! Tlong sekolong!
> Tshepe e a bitsa, tshepe e a bitsa,
> Di-thu-tong, di-thu-tong . . ."

Then he wiped his nose with the back of his hand. "Or perhaps you sang stupid baby songs about how nice it was to go to the old farm school," he taunted.

"Ma . . ." Edward said. Adam could see him clenching his fists.

"Come and wash your feet," Ma intervened before he could speak again. "Adam, you fetch the water from the tap. Magdalene, bring the jug of hot water, but first ask Mama Dora if you may have some of the water in the pot. Fill Mama Dora's pot to the brim again so that everyone can have hot water."

The small zinc bath hung on a nail against the wall in a corner of the room that Ma shared with Mama Dora and the girls. Edward had knocked the nail for the bath into the wall.

There was no room to store their other things. Everything they had brought from Dr. Marx's farm was still either in cardboard boxes or in Ntate's trunk, under the bed. Every time Ma wanted something, she had to drag the boxes and the trunk from under the bed. But it didn't seem likely that Mama Dora would shift any of her things. As long as they stayed in Mama Dora's house, they would have to make do.

"Let's wash Evon first, as she's quiet now," said Ma when Magdalene arrived with the jug of hot water. "Careful, *ausi*, you'll burn yourself! Put down the jug!"

Adam lit the candle to provide a little light. Mama Dora didn't like them to use the lamp too often. "I suppose we can close the door," he said, and glanced into the other room to check whether he had been overheard. "Just while we're washing our feet?"

"Then they'll think we're whispering about them in the dark again," said Edward. "Give Evon to me. I'll wash her. You sit down on the bed, Ma." He was still angry, but his mother's gentle voice had softened his mood. Edward could never remain angry when Ma spoke gently.

"Yes," said Maria. "Ma must sit down. Ma is very fat now."

Evon started whimpering, but Magdalene was quick to comfort her. "There we are . . . there we are . . . the first foot is clean. And the second foot . . . There we are! Let me wipe your face, as well. You look like shoe-box baby. Sefanya and the others will think Ma found you in a shoe box on the doorstep. Y-e-e-s . . . there are shoe-box babies. They're the ones with dirty faces."

Evon was actually standing quietly, her small feet in the bath water, her head to one side, as she listened to Magdalene.

Adam stared at them and something burned inside him. He remembered Ntate under the thresher, but stopped himself from thinking about it. "I wish we had our own place," he said. "Even if it were as small as this room. It's impossible to keep on living like this, with Mama Dora's children."

"Perhaps they think the same about us," said Ma slowly. "Mama Dora's children are big — she doesn't want to be bothered with little ones anymore. And there are too many of us in the house."

"You would've been different if it had been you who had to take in a crowd of kids like us," said Edward, starting to dry Evon's legs. "You always say our people struggle together to get through the tough times."

"Mama Dora has a kind heart," Ma said softly. "She's always had a kind heart. But things are getting too much for her. She has such a hard job, and then she still has to care for a crowd of visitors in her house. Perhaps it would be better if Mama Dora could work for private people again. All the women who work at Rentoclean Services complain about the amount of work."

"She's got pretty clothes for her work," said Magdalene. "I like those red dresses with the little caps."

"They're not dresses," said Edward disdainfully. "They're red smocks. All the women who work for Rentoclean wear smocks like those."

"Perhaps one of these days your mother will also wear a uniform like that," said Ma, getting up heavily. "After the birth of the baby I'll have to start working again. We can't live on only Adam's newspaper money."

"But not at Rentoclean," Adam said. "I see what happens to Mama Dora's pay envelopes. Every day the people who she's worked for must put a lot of money in the envelope. And what does Mama Dora get? Not even half. Rentoclean takes almost everything!"

"But we can't live on just your newspaper money," Ma said again. "And in any case, Ntate wouldn't have approved of your spending so little time on your schoolbooks, Adam. Ntate always had such great plans for you."

"I might as well start selling newspapers, too," Edward said suddenly. "What's the point in going to school if I have to come home in the middle of the day?"

Ma opened Evon's blanket, turned her on her side, and patted her bottom to persuade her to sleep. But Adam saw her frown as she looked back at Edward.

14

"You'll go to school as long as the school doors are open, Edward," she said sternly. "I don't want to hear that you're hanging around with good-for-nothings. If other children want to make trouble, you stay away from them. I don't want to see a police van picking you up and taking you away."

"I've had nothing to do with the trouble at school, Ma," Edward said grumpily. "I'm just saying!"

Here it goes again, Adam thought. The yellow candlelight is so pretty and Evon is quiet, sucking her thumb. You talk about red smocks and caps and newspaper money . . . and suddenly there's trouble once more. In this house troubles have little troubles: as soon as you think there are more than enough, even more appear. And then Ma speaks to me as though she thinks I can advise her, as though I'm Ntate now. But she doesn't know . . . If I can't think of a plan, we'll be without the newspaper money, as well, next week. That is the biggest problem of all. And those Casspirs rumbling in the night tell me it's not just a rumor. The biggest trouble still lies ahead.

chapter 2

Samuel Pebane had a racing bike with curved handlebars like the horns of a billygoat. Ntate's old black bicycle always felt as slow as a donkey cart when Adam saw Samuel pedaling ahead, his pedals whizzing past the chain. But that morning, Samuel rode next to Adam. He took no notice of the honking buses and cars that roared past him on the tarred road.

"What are you going to do?" he yelled above the noise of the traffic, chewing gum as if to give him strength for the steep incline. "My father says . . . we must tell old Labuschagne . . . we'll sell newspapers again . . . after the trouble. . . . My father says . . . he's not going to have his house burned down . . . for a pile of newspapers."

"I don't know what I'm going to do," Adam gasped, trying to look behind him; he could swear that his rear tire was flat again. And the pump was at home — Paul the Pest had borrowed it and not returned it. "How can I tell my mother . . . things like that . . . right now?"

"But you'll have to," said Samuel as he kneaded

the gum with his teeth. "It's no problem . . . going to work. It's coming home at night. When you come back . . . and want to go home . . . they lie in wait for you . . . and you're finished. They'll . . . burn down your house! My father says so. It's no joke."

"This tire is flat again," said Adam. He felt like screaming. "And my pump — "

"Take mine," said Samuel, dragging his foot on the tar to stop his bike. "You should've patched that puncture long ago."

But Samuel, there's no money for patches, Adam wanted to tell him. There's no money for anything. If your shirt collar is frayed, you keep on wearing it, the loose threads tickling the back of your neck. Edward's shoes gaped like open mouths, the soles like tongues, the nails like teeth. But he still had to keep on wearing them.

"Hold the bike," said Samuel. "I'll pump. If we put the bike down, these cars will kill me. Phew! You can die from the exhaust fumes of these trucks!"

Adam held the bike and watched Samuel's thin arms pumping. And suddenly, probably because the tire went flat so often, the words came tumbling out. "Samuel — what's the crossest you've ever been in your life?"

Samuel looked up, and for a few seconds his jaws stopped moving. "The crossest I've ever been? Why do you want to know?"

"Because," said Adam. A truck roared past them

and he breathed out all the air in his lungs so that he wouldn't swallow the black diesel fumes. "Go on, tell me. I just want to know."

Samuel started pumping again, faster and faster. "I'm cross every day of my life," he said. "Cross at my eldest sister. She gets home early, but she thinks she's important. She does nothing, nothing at all! I have to cook the food before my father gets home and I get beaten if the meat is tough. All she does is complain to my father because I'm out on the streets late at night. When my mother comes home from Welkom — *when* she gets time off — it's the first thing my sister tells her." He swallowed, testing the tire with his fingers. "I'm not a woman; it's a girl's job to make food when your mother works somewhere else. The day is coming when I'm going to say something."

"I wish I could be cross like that," said Adam, and the stone in his chest became heavier and heavier. "I'm terribly cross, Samuel."

"Who with?" asked Samuel, straightening his back. "The tire is better, but it'll give trouble again — today, probably. You can hear it losing air."

"I think I'm angry with . . . Modimo," said Adam, and suddenly, with the Saturday morning traffic roaring past him and the night smoke still hanging over Bochabela behind him, he felt so lonely and so awful that it no longer mattered that he had said it.

"With . . . Modimo?" he heard Samuel asking. "Are you crazy?"

18

"No," said Adam, and went on, his voice becoming shriller and shriller. "But . . . okay, you also go to church. They tell us you only have to pray and Modimo will help you. I've been praying for a long time, Samuel, a long time. At first that woman we're staying with was friendly. But now she's never kind anymore. At first my mother could work, but now she's going to have a baby—now she spends all her time lying down. Then I said: 'Never mind, Ma, everything will be fine because I found work at the newspaper.' And now? Now those people hang around the road to Phameng and they say they'll burn down everything if we go to work. Is that how Modimo answers prayers?"

Samuel handed him the bike. "*Auk*," he said, very slowly. He frowned and seemed to be searching for words. "Perhaps . . . perhaps it'll be better once your mother has the baby."

"That's when it's going to be the worst," said Adam, realizing how difficult he must sound. "There's not a single piece of clothing for that child. I was going to buy some with this month's newspaper money. And now I might have to stay away from work. What are we going to do if those people stop me from working?"

"Look," said Samuel, hopping on one leg before mounting his bike. "With those people and their necklaces, I'm taking no chances. My father says we must just keep our mouths shut, then we won't be standing there burning with a tire around our shoulders. I'm going to keep my trap shut!"

19

They rode along the tarred road in front of the smoke-blackened underpass. Adam felt as though they were traveling in a huge cage, with the electric cables strung overhead, the Bloemfontein East railway junction to his right, and a high brown wall to his left. It was impossible to talk here, with the cars roaring down the underpass and a train rumbling over the tracks.

There was a dense crowd of people on their way to work; like busy ants they scurried across the narrow pedestrian crossing behind the soot-blackened railings.

Beyond the underpass, things improved. Shopkeepers were removing the security gates and bars from the windows and chaining goods to the shop verandahs. Adam smelled vetkoek. The vetkoek seller was early today with her vetkoek stuffed with minced meat.

"My stomach's grumbling," Samuel said over his shoulder. "Wish I had mon-e-e-e-y!"

"You've got money," Adam yelled at him. "You're just mean, man!"

He knew what Samuel did with his money: he put all the coins in a jam jar with a screw top. He was saving up for one of the expensive soccer balls in the window of the sports shop. It was easy for Samuel to save; his mother worked for an attorney's wife in Welkom and earned a lot of money. And his father had been working at the Mercedes garage for years. He was good at his job and was well paid for it.

Directly opposite the four power-station towers they

had to turn toward the city. But the traffic light was red and there was time to listen to the swish of water pouring from the towers and to gaze, open-mouthed, as the tower birds took flight. The towers belched thick clouds of blue-white smoke from their open throats. If you narrowed your eyes, they looked like two fat and two thin giants puffing smoke into the blue of the sky. Around the giants, the tower birds soared at will. They seemed to be playing a game with the fumes, diving through holes where the air was still clean.

"I wonder if they live in the towers," Adam said, still looking up. "I don't see any nests."

"It must be nice and warm in winter," said Samuel, and he started pedaling again because the light had changed. "To get that much smoke you must burn a whole year's supply of coal."

The city center was already quite busy and they had to ride single file to stay out of the way of the buses. But when they had cleared the city traffic, Voortrekker Street was quieter and some of the time Samuel could ride next to Adam.

"There was a sparrow's nest in our classroom at the farm school," Adam reminisced, still thinking about the birds at the power station. "Did I tell you, Samuel?"

"Inside the classroom?" asked Samuel disbelievingly.

"Yes. He knew where to fly out: one of the windows

was broken. Sometimes he came inside while we were in class. We always looked to see what he had brought: a feather . . . a piece of string . . . dry grass. We wanted him to take a mate and have babies."

"And did he?" Samuel was interested.

"Him?" Adam laughed. "Not a chance. He liked living alone."

"It sounds as though it was a nice school," said Samuel and blew a bubble. "Or wasn't it?"

"It was a bit cold in winter," Adam remembered. "Dr. Marx always promised that he'd put in new windowpanes, but he never did. But otherwise it was very nice."

I can remember every plant on that piece of school ground, Adam thought as he pedaled. There was a hole near the soccer goalposts, and when it rained, it filled with water, and then the mosquitoes came. Those mosquitoes had a good sense of smell; they were real bloodsuckers. They came into the classroom in broad daylight and stung us until we were covered in bumps.

The blackboard hung from nails. In some places the surface was so worn that the chalk wouldn't write there anymore. Titchere, who taught them, had stuck pictures taken from magazines on the walls. Under every picture there was a caption to help you learn English quickly. One of the captions had a lovely

singing sound and the children sang it like a gospel
song:

> Paying at ease . . .
> Living in style . . .

"Pay-hing . . ." the children sang. "Pay-hing at
eazzzzzzzz . . . Liiiiving in staaa-heel . . ."

There were duwweltjies all around the school. From
October onward everyone cried and swore about the
duwweltjies. From October you could see children
jumping from one leg to another, schoolbooks in plastic
bags under their arms, their faces screwed up with pain.
But one morning in September, when the duwweltjies
were still yellow with flowers, Titchere brought pictures to school.

He told them they were pictures of Holland, a country very far away, farther even than the sea. The pictures showed windmills and wooden shoes and flowers
on long stems. "Holland is a pretty country," Titchere
said and held up the pictures so that everyone could
see them. "That's where these flowers come from."
He held up a picture of one of the long-stemmed flowers. "Edward, can you remember the English name for
these flowers?"

"Tulops," said Edward quickly.

"Tu-*lips*," Titchere corrected him. "Say it again,
Edward."

"Tulops," Edward repeated before suddenly asking

the pressing question: "Titchere, do they plant those flowers?"

"Yes, they plant them."

"We don't plant anything and we have many more," said Edward, gesturing toward the fields. "Just look outside!"

All heads turned and it was true: as far as the eye could see it was green and yellow. From field to field, from east to west, there were yellow duwweltjies. You could stare and stare outside and your eyes would never grow tired.

"But those are duwweltjies, not tulops," Titchere said.

It was Adam who corrected him: "Tu-*lips*, Titchere!" The children laughed and Titchere's face darkened, though, finally, he was forced to laugh, too.

Shortly after the yellow flowers came, Ntate and the others had to start plowing. All the duwweltjies had to be plowed under before their thorns appeared. Then the smell of the veld was at its lushest: the smell of earth being turned, the smell of the deep soil that was brought to the top. And the duwweltjies were buried alive; the duwweltjies were covered in red earth . . . until the rains came and they grew again, green with yellow flowers, like something that could never die.

"Hey-ey!" Samuel called over his shoulder. "Are you asleep, Adam?"

Indeed, the traffic light had changed to green. But for a brief moment Adam sat staring at the green light and for that moment his head was in a whirl. It's the green of September, he thought, before he automatically started pedaling again. The green of the traffic light is the green of the duwweltjies before they flower.

Old Labuschagne's face was small, and what he had was hidden behind black-framed glasses and a black moustache like a broom. Everything about old Labuschagne was black: the frame of his glasses, his moustache, his fingernails, his polo-neck sweater. It seemed as if newspaper ink had made Labuschagne black. Adam had never seen him in anything else except the polo-neck sweater. When you saw him for the first time, you expected him to have a deep voice, a voice to match the black hairs that grew on the back of his hands and out of his ears. But old Labuschagne sounded like a goat.

"Be quiet!" old Labuschagne bleated, a pile of Saturday newspapers gripped in his woolly hands. "Maerman . . . Tarzan! Who's speaking? You or me?"

"It's the master who's speaking," said Willem Maerman in a sanctimonious voice.

"Lesten," said old Labuschagne. When he spoke, his mouth twisted, flattening all his vowel sounds.

"Lesten, I hear you've had troubles again. Are you going to be here next week or not?"

"As though it's us causing the troubles," Samuel muttered to Adam.

"It's next Saturday and Sunday that there'll be trouble, master," said Petrus Tlokane, who stood at the front of the group. "There are people who say they're going to wait for us along the road, and if they catch us coming from work, they'll burn our houses."

Old Labuschagne looked uncomprehending, his face growing even smaller. "You make it very difficult for me," he said. "Are you all going to stay away?"

"The boys from Opkoms and Heidedal won't stay away, master," said Willem Maerman. "Nothing like that's happening in our townships." He added softly, "At least, not yet."

"I'll simply have to put the youngsters from the Children's Home on your corners," said old Labuschagne, looking at the group. "If it goes on like this, I'll have to fix it so that they replace you every weekend."

The newspaper sellers grumbled amongst themselves; it sounded as though a swarm of bees had moved into the hall. "Quiet!" old Labuschagne bleated, his woolly hands opening and closing, opening and closing on the newspaper pile. "Or do you want to *tjaila* right now?"

"Master, what are you going to do with the money,

master?" Samuel suddenly asked loudly. Adam's head jerked. He hadn't expected anyone to ask such a question.

"What do you mean, what am I going to do with what money?" asked old Labuschagne, and his Adam's apple grew bigger and bonier. "You can't be paid for newspapers you haven't sold."

"We won't stay away on purpose, master," said Samuel, hanging his head, embarrassed.

Old Labuschagne wrinkled his nose to push up his glasses. "If the youngsters from the Children's Home get the newspapers sold on Saturday and Sunday, they'll get the money and that's that!" he bleated.

Adam swallowed convulsively, then asked: "And if we're here, master?"

Old Labuschagne stared at him as if he were a piece of rag dug up by a dog. "If you're here to sell *Focus*," he said after a long time, "you'll be paid. As always." He took his list and began reading out the points of sale: "Andries Pretorius Street: Central School . . . Andries Pretorius Street: top end . . . Zastron Street: lower end . . . Kentucky . . . Hypermarket . . . Parkway Police Station . . ." Willem Maerman stood next to him in the cubicle with the piles of newspapers. As Labuschagne called out the names and the sellers answered, Willem pushed the piles over the counter.

"Parkway Police Station," old Labuschagne repeated.

"That's okay, master," said Willem and shot the pile in Adam's direction. "It's me and Adam and Taffie, and old Hansie."

"National Hospital," old Labuschagne read, his finger on the list. But Willem Maerman was standing with his hand in the air.

"Master, 'scuse me for interrupting, but master will have to put old Hansie with someone else. At that intersection where we work, we can't cope with a man who works in slow motion, master." He gestured impatiently. "All the customers from the Hypermarket pass there, and then there are the people from De Wet and Fauna and Uitsig—"

"Old Hansie's not that slow," Taffie Venter said loudly. "Willem just wants Tarzan back on his corner."

They all turned to look at old Hansie. He was seventy years old and the left lens of his glasses was cracked, perhaps by a pebble sent flying by a passing car. To see properly he had to hold his head at an angle so that his eyes could focus through an unbroken piece of the lens. Old Hansie was growing through his hair, said Willem Maerman, but the bald patch wasn't used to the sun yet. It seemed as though old Hansie had two kinds of skin: the soft, tender skin of the bald patch and the old, wrinkled turkey skin of his neck.

None of the other newspaper sellers knew why old Hansie sold newspapers. After all, whites took their old people to old-age homes — old white people lived in special buildings, sitting at windows, staring longingly, never speaking. And those who were strong, like old Hansie, put on white trousers and stuck white hats on their bald heads and played bowls on the bowling green near Central School.

"I'll grease my joints, sir," said old Hansie, peering through the unbroken part of his lens. "I had a bit of flu, that's all. Nothing serious."

"I don't like lame ducks," Willem Maerman mumbled. "If a man works on my corner, I don't want to have to carry him."

Old Hansie wanted to say something, but Taffie Venter motioned him to keep quiet. Taffie's nails were broken down to the quick and his white hair looked like grass around his ears, but the newspaper sellers were willing to listen to him. Samuel said that Taffie Venter had a better head on his shoulders than old Labuschagne.

The central area sellers received their newspapers and scurried off to the minibuses. "Slow-ly! Slow-ly!" old Labuschagne bleated from the cubicle. "Don't break the place down, you hear me?" Adam felt in his pocket; he hoped he hadn't lost the piece of string. It was still there, halfway through the hole in his pocket. It was easier to sling the whole pile of newspapers over the string at the fold, and to sell them from the top. If you forgot the string at home and had to carry the newspapers under your arm, they started sliding out just when you were at your busiest. Or the wind lifted the top one and blew the pages all over the place.

"Oh, no," said Samuel. "I forgot my string at home!"

"Me, too," said old Hansie.

"Bad luck," said Willem Maerman, next to Adam. "Get in, Hansie — if you want to work for me, you must have all your tools. I won't take any nonsense. Come on, Adam, the minibus won't wait for you boys to finish talking. Move it!"

"See you," said Samuel, and started running in the direction of the Andries Pretorius Street minibus.

"Do you have a knife?" Adam asked. "My string is long enough. You can have half."

"Broken glass will do," said Samuel and grabbed a piece from the gutter. Deftly he cut the string in two and pushed half into his pocket. "I owe you one, Adam."

The minibus always threw you around; you had to sit with your legs firmly planted on either side of the pile of newspapers. Willem Maerman and Taffie took turns jumping out at the cafés where they delivered newspapers and waited for the receipts to be signed. Two rands extra, Adam thought. Two rands extra, just for jumping in and out! Why doesn't anyone ever notice me? I'll never be anyone's favorite. Samuel says it's Willem's loud voice that gets him all the extra little money-making jobs.

Modimo, where am I going to find the money to help Ma? The new baby is almost here and we don't have a thing in the house. Nothing. And if we're not allowed to come to work next week . . .

Tarzan was entertaining them again, and the newspaper sellers were yelling with laughter. He pushed up the sleeve of his tattered T-shirt, flexed his muscles, and sang over the droning of the minibus:

> "I am Tarzan, Tarzan of the jungle,
> Neither Ma nor Pa have I.
> I am Tarzan, Tarzan of the *bos*,
> And I sell *Focus* for *lekker kos*.
> Come on, master, come on, madam,
> Bring your wallet closer—
> Come take your paper from my grip
> And how about a nice fat tip . . . ?"

"Parkway!" the driver called from the front. "Old Hansie, are you dozing again? You should've been out by now, old man!"

"Watch your step, Uncle Hansie," Taffie warned. "Look at the way they're driving this morning."

Adam tied the string behind his neck and hung his newspapers from it. He was still adjusting the top copy when the first motorist held out a two-rand note for a newspaper.

Adam took the money and handed over a paper.

"My change?" said the man behind the wheel. "Come on, man!"

"Don't you have any loose change, master?" Adam asked and he knew that the day was off to a bad start. "We've only just started, master. We don't have any change yet."

"Don't they give you change at the newspaper office?" The man's shoulders jerked with annoyance as he took back the two-rand note.

"No, master, we have to collect change ourselves."

Suddenly Adam thought about Tarzan's sales pitch. Supposing I asked the man for a nice fat tip? *Bring your wallet closer, come take your paper from my grip.* . . .

"Are you lying to me?" he heard the fat man ask.

"No, master — why, master?" He was frightened because the man looked angry.

"Why are you grinning all over your face?"

The light changed and the man prepared to drive off. Adam saw what was coming and he tried to prevent it from happening. "Master, please, master — you still owe me fifty cents, master."

"See that you have change next time," the man shouted as he drove off. "Waste my time like that . . ." Adam heard no more because of the stream of cars roaring past.

Old Hansie waited with him on the sidewalk. His newspapers lay at his feet and his glasses were half off his nose. "A real pig," he said and jerked his head in the direction of the passing cars. "Luckily, it's only fifty cents. One Sunday morning a couple of boys drove away with four newspapers without paying, here, on this very corner. I had to pay in. There's no point in explaining."

Adam saw the dust devil approaching, but all he could think of was the fifty cents. It was only when the wind lifted old Hansie's newspapers and Willem Maerman shouted from across the road that the old man realized that he should have done something to prevent this from happening.

"There go your newspapers!" Willem Maerman yelled. "For heaven's sake, Hansie, where are your hands?"

"Stay there, Uncle Hansie," Taffie Venter called. "You'll wind up under the cars. I'll come and help—"

"You stay right here!" Willem Maerman shouted. "Let Adam and his big mouth run! Standing there talking when he should be working . . ."

Adam heard them calling as he chased the newspaper pages. They ballooned and gusted; he saw the center spread jerk free of the bundle, open in the wind, and begin to fly. It looks just like a bird, he thought. A black-and-white bird, with limp, rectangular wings . . .

But it was a useless bird—it simply fluttered down again. With a shudder of its paper wings it dived against the windshield of an oncoming car and lay there, the tip of its wing caught under the windshield wiper. The driver rammed on the brakes, but the large car skidded over the white line. Horns started blaring and there was a screaming of brakes. The piece of newspaper had halted the whole stream of traffic.

For a moment Adam stared, mesmerized, at the sheet of newspaper.

This thing . . . was alive, he thought wildly. Just for a few seconds, it lived and flew like a wild thing, its wings filled and covered with black ink. Suddenly he heard the blare of horns, and life as well as fear flooded into his legs again. He licked his dry lips and ran to the front car.

"You . . . stupid!" the driver shouted at him. "What if we'd had an accident, hey? What's wrong with you? Why can't you hold down your newspapers?"

"I'm sorry, sir," Adam heard old Hansie behind him. "It wasn't — "

"What's your name?" the driver asked. "Speak up, you idiot!"

"A . . . A . . ." Adam stuttered.

"Andrew," said old Hansie. "His name is Andrew Sekoene, sir."

"Thanks," said the man. "I'm going to report you, you fool. Now, remove that piece of paper!"

Adam grabbed the piece of newspaper, his legs feeling as weak as they had done when he'd nearly died of the runs. The motorists honked, and he stood back so that the traffic could move again. But the last thing he saw as the angry driver drove away was a clenched fist waving in his direction.

"What a business!" said old Hansie, sighing as he took the sheet of newspaper from Adam. "I'm sorry, Adam. He should've shouted at me. Maybe they're right about me and this job."

"*Auk*," was all that Adam could say. He looked around. The sky seemed pale, as though the smoke from all four power-station towers had smothered everything. Why must I work here? he wondered, over and over again. Why must I keep my mouth shut while other people . . .

"I'm sorry," old Hansie said again. "It was my fault."

"It wasn't really," said Adam, trying to swallow the tears in his throat. "The . . . piece of newspaper looked . . . like a bird," he said. "Like a . . . darn bird that flew against that man's windshield and then . . . just lay there . . . dead."

"Yes, it did," said old Hansie. "If you don't put a stone on your newspapers, they just start flying."

"Like birds," Adam said quietly. "With black ink for blood."

chapter 3

After half-past twelve you could forget about selling any newspapers. All the cars that passed were loaded with plastic bags filled with groceries, bags of dogfood, stuff for the garden; and in the back, whining children with sticky mouths. Everyone was on the way home after a morning spent at the Hypermarket, and no one gave the newspaper placards a second glance.

Old Hansie unfastened the string of his orange safety jacket and pulled it over his head. "This little apron is getting pretty warm, now," he said and bent down to count his unsold newspapers. "Well, my goodness," he said. "If my feet don't carry me to my grave before evening, it'll be only eight days to the big day."

"What big day?" Adam asked, counting the four newspapers remaining on his string as though he didn't know perfectly well there were four left. If only someone would drive past and say: "Hey, give me four, will you?"

"Next Saturday we're having a ceremony for war veterans," said old Hansie.

Adam wanted to ask about it, but the minibus had stopped across the road and they had to run. Old Hansie was tired. You could see how he dragged his feet.

"Now for a big piece of polony," said Tarzan, who was already in the minibus. "My stomach is aching with hunger."

"Today I'm going to buy myself a meat pie," said Willem Maerman, and he yawned. "I don't know how I'm going to stay awake until tonight, boys."

Neither do I, Adam thought. I'm dead on my feet. Who can sleep with Evon whining about her ear? And then Sefanya comes home after midnight and Mama Dora kicks up a row. And Ma didn't even get up this morning. She didn't have the strength to get up and make the putu.

His stomach churned again. In the gray light, old Hansie was showing his war scar to Tarzan and Willem and Taffie. His trouser leg was pulled up and Adam saw that he wore red-and-green-striped socks. But Adam didn't want to look. His head was filled with thoughts of the baby about to be born and the house that was already too full.

We'll have to let the child sleep in one of the boxes, he thought suddenly. It's the only room there is. He found this so funny that he gurgled. Luckily the noise of the engine was loud and no one heard him.

The minibus that Samuel and the others traveled in was already parked under the lean-to and, as usual,

Samuel was waiting on the steps in front of the security office. But when he got out, Adam saw that something must have happened: Samuel's face looked excited.

"Adam!" Samuel called. "Let old Hansie pay in for you — I've got something to tell you."

Adam's flesh crawled. Brusquely he handed the money to old Hansie, his head spinning. Those people waiting for us on the road to Phameng . . . But it couldn't be that; that wasn't until next week. They couldn't have started punishing people for going to work today? Or had there been a fire again — one of the sudden fires they'd had recently?

"What's the matter?" he asked when he reached Samuel.

"We just got here, right?" said Samuel and nearly choked on his own spittle. "Our bus was here first, right? Well, then the phone rang in the office there and old Ox came out and said that someone had been trying to get you on the phone for ages. You weren't here so I went — "

"And?" Adam asked. His legs felt weak again. For one awful moment he saw the white flesh of the potato bursting through the broken skin. If something was wrong with Ma . . . Or had the people in the Casspirs grabbed Sefanya? Mama Dora often whispered to Ma about Sefanya. Sefanya had the wrong friends and he came home late at night. . . .

"It was Edward who wanted to speak to you," said

Samuel. "He was phoning from a public phone. He said your mother had gone to the hospital and that the child was born — but it's . . . it's *twins.*"

Adam stood there stunned, as though Samuel had hit him over the head with a hubcap. He couldn't utter a word, and something seemed to be stuck in his throat. Eventually, after swallowing a few times, he managed to gasp: "What did you say, Samuel? Twins? Two babies? Are you sure that's what Edward said?"

"You heard me," said Samuel, and he wasn't smiling. "Edward says your little sister is shouting the house down — she wants your mother and there's something wrong with her ear. He says you must come home otherwise he'll throttle . . . otherwise he'll do something to her. She's crying for you, too."

Silently, Adam stared at Samuel.

"Your mother won't stay in the hospital for long," said Samuel. "I know — my eldest sister came home on the second day."

"What good will it do if my mother comes home quickly?" Adam said, wanting to scream. "What are we going to do with the babies? Must we wrap them in Mama Dora's dishrags and put them in the boxes under the bed? They've got nothing, Samuel, nothing."

"What do you mean, nothing?"

"Nothing," said Adam. "My mother had to buy schoolbooks when we moved to town from the farm. We had to have new clothes for the school here . . .

My mother has to pay Mama Dora for food and paraffin
. . . I was going to buy clothes for the child this month
with my newspaper money. But now the child — the
children have come early. And nothing is ready for
them."

"Don't you have any money — not even for a few
diapers?" Samuel asked disbelievingly.

"All I have is this," said Adam and jingled the coins
in the pocket that wasn't torn. "I can barely buy polony
with it!"

"Aren't you hungry?" Samuel asked and jerked his
head in the direction of the café, where a crowd of
newspaper sellers still hung about.

"No," said Adam. "In any case, I have to go. I
know what my little sister must be doing by now —
yelling so hard that you can see halfway down her
throat. Edward won't be able to keep her quiet. He
gets crosser and crosser and then he shakes her and
yells in her ear. The more he shakes and yells, the
harder Evon screams."

They saw old Hansie approaching, but it was only
when he spoke that they realized he wasn't simply
shuffling past them. "Adam, you added up wrongly:
you still owe eighty cents."

"Eighty cents!" said Samuel. "Can't you leave
Adam alone? Look at his face!"

Old Hansie looked carefully at Adam's face. "Come
on, my boy, why are you looking like that? Okay, it
was a bad day — "

"His mother had twins," said Samuel. "Today."

Old Hansie's jaw dropped. "But that's . . . that's good news!" he said after a while. "I don't understand. The Lord gives your mother two children, and you look as though the world has come to an end!"

"I'm sure I don't look that bad," said Adam. "But how would you like to have two children all at once?"

"He can't, Adam," said Samuel dryly. "Only women can have children."

Adam took eighty cents from his handkerchief and pressed it into Hansie's hand. "There's the eighty cents. I don't have time to wait around the office. I have to go home because my sister has earache."

"*Tsamaya hantle* — go well," Samuel said weakly.

"*Sala hantle* — stay well," said Adam. But he didn't really mean it. He was so confused that he was even angry with Samuel.

chapter 4

It was only five kilometers from the center of the city to where the dirt road turned off the tarred road toward Phameng, but that day it felt to Adam like fifty.

My legs feel like bags filled with stones, Adam thought, as he rode through the underpass. Why did the road seem endless? He cycled past the prison, past the deserted bus terminus where the fruit and vegetable vendors sat, past Pelonomi Hospital where the ambulances stood waiting, in case of accident or illness.

It was only when he had almost passed the hospital that he remembered: Ma was there! With the child who had turned into twins. Who had taken her to the hospital? She could hardly have walked — not with a body that looked as though it was ready to burst. The ambulance must have fetched her. Or a taxi.

And that costs money as well, he thought helplessly. I *can't* stay away next week! If old Labuschagne gives my place to the kids from the Children's Home and I lose my corner . . .

His thoughts whirled around aimlessly; they kept butting into a brick wall. If I could just get out of

Phameng without their seeing me . . . if I could hide somewhere in the city, sell the newspapers, and hide again until they're not lying in wait any longer . . . They won't check the city to see who's working. They'll be on the streets of the township all day long, beating up the people who come home from work and stealing from them. I should not go back, that's all. There are so many children in Phameng that they would hardly know that one particular newspaper seller was hiding in the city.

Perhaps he could sleep in an empty house. Old Hansie said there were many empty houses in Long Street — people had moved away because of the soot from the trains. Or on one of the sites where they were building cluster houses. The tightly packed little houses were going up everywhere. In King Edward Street they were demolishing all the old houses and building cluster upon cluster of small houses. If he could manage to get in between the houses, he might even be able to hide from the night watchmen. All they did was huddle closer to their fires where it was warm.

He pedaled until his muscles ached. A memory was nibbling at his mind. After the students' intervarsity match, *Focus* had carried a big front-page story: *Students sleep in church. Action considered.* Adam gradually remembered more and more: the beer cans left lying around, the sexton who'd found them. Were all churches open at night?

Modimo! he thought, feeling lightheaded because of

43

his empty stomach. Modimo, I'm trapped. Everything has become too much, I feel as though I'm in a cage, Modimo!

Ntate, his father, had believed in prayer. Once a day they all had to sit quietly while Ntate prayed. Ntate prayed about everything: that the wind would bring rain, that the children would be obedient, that Titchere would explain the word of the Lord to them in the right way.

Sometimes, Adam remembered, Modimo had listened — at least to Ntate. Most of the time the wind had brought rain. And Titchere was serious about the word. The only problem was that the children weren't obedient.

"Modimo!" Adam prayed. He knew that Ntate wouldn't have been satisfied with this kind of prayer, but he had no choice. "Modimo, give me a plan!"

He rode over the ground where the cattle grazed. The back mudguard of Ntate's old bike rattled as if it was about to fall off and join all the other pieces of iron and broken glass on the barren veld. Magdalene collected pieces of glass; she was always picking up all kinds of glass on the cattle's grazing field.

At the hotel he turned up Bataung Street, his feet pedaling more slowly. He recognized the houses — he passed there every day. In front of 4628, the little ones had dragged an old tin bath into the street. Their noses running, they sat in the cold, playing in the water, with pieces of wood and screw-top bottlecaps for boats. Adam was about to ride past, but a little voice from the group called out: *"Ke aubuti! E-hei, Adam!* — It's my brother! Hey, Adam!"

Who on earth . . .

It was Maria. Her wet dress, torn at the shoulder, clung to her legs. Her jersey was pulled on back to front.

"Maria!" Adam exploded. "When Ma comes home, she'll warm your backside!"

She clambered up in front of him and he shivered from the touch of her wet, cold little body. "Ma is home," she said indignantly, and waved to the children round the bath like the wife of a chief. "Evon's ear is sore and Ma has brought more children home. But they're small — very small! I waited here to tell you."

"Ma brought . . . more children home?" Adam could barely utter the words. "Where is Ma? I thought she was in Pelonomi Hospital!"

Maria fidgeted on the front of the bike and tried to ring the bell. "Why is it so brown?" she asked. "Why is the bell so brown?"

"Because it's rusty," he said, annoyed. "Maria! Tell me! How can Ma be at home when . . . if she had the child — the babies — this morning?" Even as he scolded her, he remembered that she was only four years old. Sighing, he removed her determined little hand from the bell. "Leave that! You'll make us fall!"

She looked up at him, her eyes large and black. "Won't fall," she said sweetly. And suddenly: "Hear Evon crying?"

There was no need for her to say it. Evon was crying so loudly that the sound carried over the backyard, over the corrugated iron and the chicken coops and the roofs of the outside latrines. When it's very dry and very hot, Adam thought confusedly, the ghost water on the roads and in the dry pans makes me feel peculiar. The ghost water shone in the sunlight but you knew there was no water, you knew the pan was dry and cracked. You couldn't stare at ghost water for long. It kept moving and shifting; ghost water made your head and your eyes shiver. And as soon as your eyes started to shiver, you became queasy, as though you had an upset stomach.

When Evon screamed, ghost water shivered in your body. It shivered through your ears and your head until it was deep inside you.

He pedaled harder. From afar he could see Magdalene sitting in front of the small gate of Mama Dora's plot. Her dress was on inside out, as though no one had helped her to dress. She was trying to put her hand over Evon's mouth. Evon looked like an angry ant — she was kicking so wildly, she seemed to have six legs.

They saw him coming and jumped up, coming to a halt just in front of the bike. Magdalene tried to tell him something, but Evon was yelling so loudly that he couldn't hear a word.

Adam lifted Maria off the bike and knelt next to Evon. "Listen," he said as quietly as possible, because when Evon's ear hurt she only listened if you spoke softly. "Now, you must cry very quietly so that I can hear what you want to say. If you cry loudly, I can't hear what you want to tell me."

"We have two babies," Magdalene shouted, but he motioned her to be quiet.

"Cry quietly now," he said to Evon and opened his arms as Ntate had always done. That had calmed her —Evon liked arms. She gave him a suspicious look, then heaved a great sob and walked into his arms. "There now, tell me," he said in a whisper, because whispering was the best way.

"Want in!" she said.

"She can't go in," said Magdalene. "Mama Dora chased us out, Adam! Only Edward's inside, working, because Mama Dora says it looks like a shebeen!" She was nearly choking with excitement. "Ma must sleep. Mama Dora doesn't want Evon in the house."

"Want in!" Evon started crying again.

"Shush, Evon," said Adam, plans rolling through his head. Sweets? Or shall I tell her that I'll buy her a doll later on? Evon had only one idea: *Popi . . . Popi . . . Ma, popi*! "Listen carefully, if you cry quietly . . ."

And suddenly, on the street, the answer appeared. Adam looked up and saw the big vehicles coming closer. At first he had to fight his own fear of the Casspirs, but now it was more important for Evon to be quiet.

"Look," he said, because he could see that the Casspirs were going to turn into Mphisi Street. "Do you see those things? They're the trucks who take away children who keep on crying. You're nice and quiet now, that's why they're driving away."

"Won't they come again?" Evon asked, her eyes huge and her face gray with fright.

"They wait behind those houses," he lied smoothly. "To listen for children who are crying."

"Then I'll run away," said Maria, and he heard her teeth chattering because of her wet clothes. "They won't catch me!"

"Then be quiet now," Adam scolded. "You can't run away from the police. They throw tear gas, and when your eyes are watering . . ."

"Then they grrrrab you!" Maria completed his sentence. Her eyes shone and her nose was dripping. Her damp clothes clung to her thin body. She'd better stay outside as well, Adam thought. Mama Dora would have a fit if Maria went in looking like that.

Evon clung to him. "Little bit in," she begged.

"I'm cold," said Maria.

But it was Magdalene who made him lose his last shred of patience.

"Adam!" she said, as though she had forgotten something important. "Adam, listen! There's something you must tell Ma. Will you? Will you tell her?"

"What?" he asked, trying to pry loose Evon's clinging hands which were dragging at his clothes. "What is it?"

"You don't want to listen."

He sighed. Her lower lip was drooping. "Go on, tell me."

"My tooth is loose," said Magdalene triumphantly. "Now, I'm going to be rich."

Adam had no energy to answer. He opened Mama Dora's front door and fled into the house. Immediately he smelled the new smell: Ma's hospital smell and the new, sweetish smell of babies.

Edward was just inside the door, a duster in his hand. "Shhh," he said. And, suddenly embarrassed: "It's Mama Dora who's making me do girl's work, because Magdalene must look after Evon."

Something must have happened: the table and chairs had been shifted and Magdalene's and the other children's blankets were rolled up and lying in a corner. There was a damp smell as though the whitewashed walls had been cleaned and hadn't yet dried.

"I must go back to the newspaper again," Adam said in a whisper. "I'll go in quietly. But how did Ma manage to come home so soon?"

"Dunno," said Edward. He looked silly and self-conscious, holding the duster. "You'd just left when

Ma said she was in pain and Mama Dora called a taxi. And she went along with Ma and came back later and said there was big trouble because there were two babies instead of one. Then I phoned you but you weren't there — "

"Yes, but how did Ma get back here?"

"In another taxi," Edward said. "She borrowed the money from Mama Dora. I saw it. She told Mama Dora she wanted to be here and nowhere else because Evon wouldn't go to sleep without her." He glanced at the other room and spoke softly: "I don't think Mama Dora would've given us food if Ma hadn't come back home. Ma knows that. It's because of the food that she came back — she knew we'd have died of hunger."

"But — " Adam realized there was no point in arguing. "I'm going to tell Ma I'm here."

He opened the door of the room, noticing the hole Sefanya and Paul's father had made, kicking it in a fit of temper. He was glad that Uncle Saul was not his father.

Ma lay quietly on the bed and Mama Dora sat in front of the small window, sewing. When the door creaked, Ma turned her head. It seemed as though she had known he would come.

"How did you manage to come home at this time of day, Adam?" she asked softly, smiling at him.

He didn't know what to say. "*Dumela*, Ma," he said and his voice cracked. "*Wena o kae*? How are

50

you?" What did you ask your mother when she was lying in bed like that? It sounded so stupid: How are you? But what else could you ask when Mama Dora sat watching you like that?

"*Nna ke teng* — I'm well," she said and while she was speaking she lifted the blanket so that he could see the two small bundles next to her on the bed.

They weren't even wrapped in matching blankets, Adam thought stupidly, but in pink and yellow blankets.

"What are they?" he asked. "I mean, are they girls or boys?"

"Haven't they told you?" asked Ma, and suddenly she looked different, almost beautiful, even though her face was so tired. "Two boys, of course!"

He bent down and carefully lifted a corner of the blanket in which the one nearest him was wrapped. He saw a pale little face with two pale pink hands that immediately started waving like the paws of a newborn rat.

"He's the eldest," said Ma softly.

"Why . . . why is he such a funny color?"

"He'll change," said Mama Dora at the window. "You also looked like that."

"He looks like Ntate," said Ma and Adam looked up quickly because her voice was so thin. He saw her fumbling in the bedding. Seeing the damp, crumpled handkerchief he handed it to her.

It was some time before he could speak again. "Then

. . . then you'll call him Jacob, won't you, Ma? After Father."

Ma pressed the hanky to her eyes. "I thought of that, too," she said after a while. "But I don't know about the other one. I didn't expect two."

Adam lifted the pink blanket and looked at the second baby for a long time. He looks like Evon, he thought. The same cross little mouth, the same high forehead. Only the color was wrong. This one looked even more like a small, wrinkled rat.

"Ma can call him . . . Esau," he said. "Like Esau and Jacob . . . in the Bible. You can see he's going to be a wild one." Suddenly he remembered the words that he'd enjoyed so much one Sunday: "He shall be a man like the wild ass."

"*Hau!*" said Mama Dora and she and Ma looked at him with wide eyes. "Where did you hear that, Adam?"

"Evangedi read it like that," he said. "Esau was a wild ass of a man — that's what the Bible says."

"*Hau*," Mama Dora said again. "That's an ugly thing the child is saying. It's the first time I hear somebody say a thing like that when he sees his brother for the first time!" She bit off a piece of thread and held the bent needle against the light. "Come on, Adam, your eyes are still strong. Come and thread the needle for me so that I can make these clothes smaller for your brothers."

He had difficulty getting the thread through the needle, but Mama Dora waited, arms akimbo, expecting him to succeed. It was only after he'd wet the thread that he managed it.

"Dirtying the thread!" said Mama Dora indignantly. "You must wash your hands when you get home, Adam. You dirty everything with that newspaper ink of yours."

"I'm pleased that you came, Adam," said Ma from the bed. "Are you going to work again tonight?"

"I must, Ma." He knew it was silly, but he felt as though he were small again and walking behind her like a shadow, part of her dress clutched in one fist.

I was stupid when I was small, he thought. I wouldn't go to sleep at night unless I held a bit of Ma's dress. I sucked my thumb and tickled my nose with a piece of her dress.

"I'll go and make some coffee," he said. "With lots of sugar."

"*Kwala monyako* — close the door!" Mama Dora's scolding voice followed Adam out of the room.

Edward looked startled when Adam came in. He was chewing something and hastily replaced the lid of a tin. But Adam was too preoccupied and worried to bother about what Edward was up to.

"The other one's name is going to be Esau," he said to Edward, taking the tin of coffee powder from the shelf. "Light the primus, please."

"Esau is an old man's name," said Edward argumentatively. "*Ntatemoholo Esau*—Grandpa Esau!"

"It's not always Grandpa Esau," Adam countered. "It's from the Bible and it suits him."

As he pumped the primus, the blue flame hissed. *Eeee-sau . . . Eeeee-sau . . . Eeeeeee-sau . . .*

chapter 5

That Saturday evening Adam and old Hansie made a fire because it was cold; winter had slipped in almost unnoticed.

Willem Maerman shouted from across the street: "What's the matter with you two? It isn't cold!" But shortly after eleven, just before the movie houses and theaters closed, he and Taffie Venter joined them round the small blaze. "The fire makes your feet feel the way hot soup feels in your belly," said Willem, standing almost in the fire. "If you have soup in your belly, you're warm!"

"If you stand on one leg like that," said old Hansie drily, "you'll be in the soup, belly and all." He laughed at his own joke and squinted through his broken glasses at the newspaper Taffie Venter was trying to read in the white glare of the streetlights. "What do they say about old Naas, Taffie?"

"Nothing much," said Taffie and opened the newspaper as though he'd paid for it. "But this is a nice photo of him — I've been looking for one like this for a long time. Wish I could keep it."

55

"You better fold up that paper right away," said Willem Maerman. "If they catch you fooling about with a newspaper . . . Hey, Adam, here's a piece about Bochabela and Phameng and Rocklands again. You want to hear?"

He didn't wait for Adam's answer but started reading in a monotone, like the buzzing of a bluebottle against a window.

"The situation in Bochabela, Phameng and Rocklands, outside Bloemfontein, is tense. Our correspondent reports that thousands of children are staying away from school because of the fear that their homes will be burned down. Workers are also being intimidated and hundreds have informed their employers that they won't be working next week. Employers in Bloemfontein have agreed that stayaway workers will not be dismissed but that they will receive no pay or compensation for the days that they are absent. . . ."

Adam listened without moving. He felt peculiar — as though he was listening to a story he didn't like; as though he wished the old man telling the story would grow sleepy and doze off before he'd finished.

"But who are the guys threatening you like this, Adam?" asked Taffie, folding the newspaper in half.

They all looked at him: old Hansie's neck was askew again as he tried to focus through the unbroken piece of lens.

"I don't know," Adam heard himself saying. "We

came to the city from the farm when my father died and we found it like this. Mama Dora — she's one of my mother's family and we're staying with her — Mama Dora said we mustn't look for trouble. If they say do this, we do it. If they tell us to go home from school, then we go home. But I'm not sure who 'they' are."

"How are you going to pass your exams if you stay away from school?" Taffie asked. "Why must you listen to them?"

"One Monday morning a child argued with those boys who chase us home," said Adam. Suddenly he seemed to hear footsteps behind him. He looked over his shoulder but it was dead quiet; all he could see were shadows on the wall.

"And then?" Willem Maerman asked.

"They necklaced his dog," said Adam. He could have sworn that the shadows were making a sound.

"Did you . . . see it?" asked Taffie.

"No, but I heard people screaming," said Adam.

"Were they crying?" asked Taffie.

Adam remembered how quiet Mama Dora's house had been. Ma and Mama Dora had cocked their heads to one side. Some of the dishwater ran down Mama Dora's sleeve; she forgot to dry the pot in her hands. Paul the Pest and Mannetjie and Moses peered though a crack in the back door, and Magdalene's hand was thrust halfway down her throat. Moments before,

Sefanya had flown through the front door and said breathlessly: "Don't let the children go outside! They're going to do a necklace—just behind our house."

"To a . . . person?" Ma asked, her hands suddenly trembling.

"To John Sethunya's dog," said Sefanya. "Because John was feisty this morning."

Then the dog whined, finding itself caught in a trap. If a dog could cry, John Sethunya's dog wept. It was quiet in Mama Dora's house, dead quiet. Outside, many voices started screaming. But it wasn't the sound of weeping, it was a yell of triumph.

"Were they crying?" Taffie insisted.

"No," said Adam, glad to see that a few cars were approaching and that the traffic lights were red. "No, they were simply yelling."

Old Labuschagne kept them cleaning up until after a quarter past one because the place was littered with torn newspaper, bread crusts, and chewing gum wrappers. The newspaper had been late because there had been a mine disaster in the Transvaal, and while they waited, everyone had eaten bread and polony and chewed gum.

Old Labuschagne was at his most dangerous when they returned after the Saturday-night sales. He'd had a few drinks, but not enough to cheer him up, and as a result he refused to let anyone leave until the whole floor had been cleaned.

When Adam and Samuel left for Phameng at half-past one, they had no strength left for conversation. At that time of night, thinking was confused. There were still many people on the streets, mostly young ones who'd had too much to drink. Riding through Phameng's streets at that time of night, it was best not to say a word. All you wanted to do was get home. There was no point in looking for trouble. You made yourself small, very small, like a cat in a strange backyard.

Already, many of the houses were dark, but there were still flickering lights — lamplight and candlelight — behind the curtains and pieces of cardboard in the windows. The night was full of shadows that jumped and crept and disappeared. Candlelight made real shadows; when a house had no electricity, dark shadows flickered in it. Mama Dora said that it cost thousands to have electricity in a house.

"Just smell," Samuel said.

Samuel said that night smells were different from day smells. Samuel said that if you put ten people in a row and blindfolded him, he could recognize each one by smell, like a bloodhound. And at night, said Samuel, Phameng smelled of smoking lamps and candlewicks and sweaty blankets and tonsils and croup. At night, Samuel said, people's breath had a different smell, and children's wet diapers, too. He's right, Adam thought. That's what you smell through the cardboard that keeps out the cold.

59

Near Samuel's turnoff, Adam suddenly stopped pedaling. "Samuel, why are the Casspirs here again?" He was overcome by a terrible fear. A fear that paralyzed him. He'd done nothing wrong, so why should he be so scared when he saw the great hulking shapes of the Casspirs?

"Where?" asked Samuel.

"There — at the hall."

"I don't know," Samuel answered abruptly. "But let's get home." He spoke hurriedly, making his bike jump over the potholes in the street as he pedaled.

At Mama Dora's house, light still shone from one small window. Adam knocked and a sleepy Sefanya opened the door. The floor was covered with bodies: both Magdalene and Maria had been moved to the front room with all their blankets and belongings. He bumped against Maria's arm and she mumbled and complained in her sleep. "Is my mother still awake?" Adam asked Sefanya.

"I suppose so," Sefanya mumbled and fell back on his blankets. "See for yourself."

By now his eyes were used to the darkness as he trod carefully over the bodies and knocked at the door of his mother's room.

"Is that you, Adam?" his mother asked.

"We had to work late, Ma."

Carefully he opened the door. Ma and Mama Dora were lying on the only bed. Mama Dora was sleeping;

her mouth was open and she was snoring gently. The babies were awake next to Ma. When he closed the door softly behind him, one of the two started a low, erratic wailing.

"They're very hungry," Ma said. "I'm glad you've come. Help me with the diapers. Quickly, Adam!"

She drew the blankets aside; the babies lay next to each other in their wraps. They were clearly angry, waving their little arms furiously. And they were drowning in two huge jackets that Adam had never seen before. They looked so disheveled that he felt like taking them by their little necks and shaking them into some kind of shape. Esau was wearing only one white sock, which made his foot look like a blob of cotton candy on a thin stick. The sock was far too big.

"Where did the clothes come from?" Adam asked.

"Borrowed. I'll have to feed him before Jacob, otherwise he'll wake the whole household."

The dry diapers were lying in a pile in front of the window. Adam found it hard to fold one. Ma took the diaper and folded it with one hand. He unfastened Esau's diaper pin, vaguely remembering how he'd done it for Evon. Then he lifted the little legs and smeared the small bottom with petroleum jelly from the half-empty jar.

Esau hung half suspended, dead quiet, his hands motionless, as though he were surprised.

"There you are," Adam said, his head spinning from

lack of sleep. "No more weeing until tomorrow, d'you hear me?"

The baby stared at him with unfocused eyes, seeing everything and nothing.

"He can't see properly," said Adam, struggling to push the diaper pin through the material.

"They can only see properly later on," his mother said.

"This pin doesn't work, Ma."

"There's soap next to the basin," she said patiently. "Stick the point of the pin in the soap, then try again."

He did so and the soap worked like magic. The pin slid through the layers of material as though there had never been a problem.

Ma unfastened her nightgown and put Esau to her breast. Jacob was dozing again, and Adam changed his diaper with ease. When he had finished, he waited to take Esau from Ma and wondered how there could be so much milk for the babies when she ate so little.

"Go to bed now," she said. "The night is old, my son."

"Will Ma be all right, now?" he asked and his voice had that strange crack again. "I can still help, Ma."

"You help more than enough," she said softly. "You're the man in the house now, Adam. You're not *moshemane* — a boy — any longer. I see you're becoming what I can call *monna* — a man." She must have thought that he didn't believe her, because she added, seriously: "I'm speaking the truth, Adam. You've lost the boy in you. You're becoming a man —I can see it."

He went to bed and all night long he dreamed. There were too many dreams.

In his dream he and Sefanya were pushing a wire car and Sefanya, in a mean mood, bent the wire. "You spoil everything!" Adam shouted at Sefanya in his dream.

But Sefanya held on and teased him: "Go on, look! Look what I've built!"

He looked, and it was a Casspir with two beer cans for headlights.

"I'll park it here, right in front of the house," Sefanya said and Adam saw that he was holding a sjambok. "If that sister of yours cries about her ear once more, I'll drive right through your house!"

In his dream Adam dropped the wire car, but Sefanya ran after him, mocking him: "Your dead Ntate couldn't spell, Adam! Everyone says your Ntate couldn't spell. Whoever heard of anyone spelling Yvonne like that? Evon, Evon, Evon. Your Ntate was stupid!"

He ran and he ran, dodging between the houses. He stumbled over broken objects and found himself caught between two outside latrines. Then, in broad daylight, the night-soil cart arrived and he smelled the dreadful smell of the pails. He hurt himself falling against a communal tap and a woman yelled at him: "That's the bad boy from the farm. It's his fault that our cows don't give milk!"

In the dream, suddenly, Ntate was sitting on an antheap on the veld in front of the hotel. One by one he was taking crumpled yellowed pages from the pockets of his overalls. "See, Adam," Ntate said to him, "you must get diplomas, too, you and Edward and Magdalene — all of you. If I didn't have the diploma from the Training College, I would've been out of work today."

Yes, but when Ntate and the diplomas were no longer there, Adam wanted to tell him, we couldn't stay on Dr. Marx's farm any longer. But he saw something moving behind the hotel and said, instead: "They're waiting for us on the streets, Ntate. I want to work, Ntate, but we're scared of the people who wait for us on the road into Phameng."

In his dream Ntate's head leaned more and more to one side, and suddenly he was wearing a pair of broken glasses. "*Tche!*" Adam shouted in the dream. "Ntate, *tche!*"

But then it wasn't Ntate any longer — it was old Hansie with the blocked nose who said: "Your mother still owes Mama Dora the money for the taxi."

On Sunday morning, Adam woke thick-headed from lack of sleep. It was still early; there was almost no sound. But the silence was broken by a large vehicle passing in the street. It sounded like a Casspir with a cold engine.

He put on his shirt and decided to take a chance; surely Mama Dora wouldn't mind if he lit the primus and made himself a mug of coffee. After all, Ma had paid for the tin of coffee powder. He felt weak with hunger.

Mannetjie peered at him through an eye swollen with sleep, but nodded off again. Sefanya simply turned over and pulled the blankets over his head. Magdalene sat up, her dress wrinkled from sleeping in it. "Adam . . ." she whispered urgently and Adam had to shush her to stop her waking Evon too.

"But I want to tell you something," Magdalene whispered and got up, clutching her blankets.

Adam caught her just before she dragged her blankets over Evon's face. His head felt so thick that he was close to falling. His ears were so blocked that he was almost deaf, and his nose was blocked too.

"Come outside!" he scolded and lifted her over Maria. "Do you want everybody to wake up?"

Opening the back door he carried her outside. It was odd to see the little plot so empty — only the bantams were pecking at the trodden earth, scratching for something to eat. One perched on Mama Dora's chair outside, as though it knew that only when the quick-tempered woman was sleeping was it cock of the walk.

Or perhaps it had jumped on Mama Dora's outside chair to see whether the Casspirs were driving away. It was so inquisitive that Adam sometimes wondered whether it could think. Not real human thoughts, but brief chicken thoughts of maize and leftover putu and rice.

"Feel here," said Magdalene and opened her mouth. "In font."

"Where?" Adam asked, wrinkling up his nose in distaste. "What's 'in font'?"

"In front," Magdalene said crossly. "Can't you see?"

"Yes, you've got a loose tooth," said Adam and dried his wet fingers on his trouser leg. "What about it?"

Her face changed as though she was listening to a story. "Adam," she said, "did you know that there really is someone called Kgatwane?"

"Who?"

"Kgatwane," she said dreamily. "He is a very old lizard who used to be a chief's son. He wanted to marry a beautiful girl but then she died and he got smaller and smaller — "

"Where did you hear this story?" he asked, surprised, and saw the little bantam cock stretch its neck as though it wanted to listen, too.

"Agnes's mother teaches at the blue-roof school. She's very clever. She told Agnes and Agnes told me.

66

But I haven't finished telling. Kgatwane got smaller and smaller from all the crying and became a lizard living among the rocks. Now, he comes out at night and he listens — he listens to children crying because of loose teeth being pulled. . . ."

"Why would he do that?" Adam asked.

"Because he cried so much himself," said Magdalene. "And do you know what he does then, Adam? He leaves something for that child at the door under a stone. Agnes got five kinds of candy: a sucker and licorice and . . . and . . . I can't remember now, but there was also a packet of those candies that have little rings."

"Tsssss," Adam said, so annoyed that he spat. "Her mother put them there."

"*Tche!*" Magdalene said, sounding as though they'd been fighting and she had pinned him down. "That's not true! Agnes showed me Kgatwane's tail . . . it was a lizard's tail. It dropped off in front of Agnes's house."

"You mustn't believe stories like that," said Adam.

She looked into his eyes and he suddenly felt uneasy. She looked as angry as Evon, as wilful as Edward, as small and powerful as Maria.

"I know Kgatwane will come," she said firmly. "I keep wiggling my tooth. And when I find my candy under that stone, then you'll be sorry. You'll be sorry for making fun of Kgatwane! I'll only give some to Ma and the babies."

When Adam rode to the newspaper printer with Samuel later that day, Samuel immediately saw that something was wrong.

"You look like a dog with a runny tummy," he said and slapped Adam on the back. "Did the babies keep you awake?" He pedaled hard. "Or are you thinking about working on Saturday? You mustn't go to work on Saturday, Adam. My sister says ugly things are happening."

"I'm not thinking about Saturday now," said Adam and looked back to where the smoke was lying like low clouds above Phameng. If he hadn't known it was Phameng, he might have thought it was a city of ghosts: no ground or trees or windows were visible. It seemed as though the hazy treetops were drifting in the smoke, as though everything was drifting, drifting — weightless and without foundation. His head felt as though it was filled with water.

"*Auk*," Samuel said next to him. "You're funny this morning." He gave a sudden laugh. "You look like my father when he talks about asparagus."

"About . . . asparagus?" Adam asked. His ears felt as if they were blocked by cottonwool. He felt more and more stupid. For the life of him he couldn't think what asparagus looked like. "Those green things — a cool, fat thing?"

"Asparagus mustn't be fat," said Samuel. "You're thinking of cucumbers. My father worked on an asparagus farm, near Ficksburg. That was before he started working at the garage here. They had to pick asparagus. There were long rows of them because you plant asparagus in raised rows, you know. My father says you bend and you pick and you bend and you pick until your back feels as though it's breaking, and when you reach the end of the row you think: now I can rest a bit. But when you look back, the asparagus at the beginning of the row are as high as your finger again. They grow behind your back. When my father has troubles he always says: 'It's asparagus time again!' "

Adam thought of Magdalene wiggling her tooth and he laughed out of sheer hopelessness. "Then it's asparagus time for me, too, Samuel!"

chapter 6

Monday morning started badly. Adam was woken by the deep droning of several Casspirs in the street; it sounded as though the big vehicles would burst through the front wall of the house. A voice was speaking over a bullhorn. It sounded like English, but Evon and Maria had started crying and he couldn't make out the words. When he jumped up, his head was still heavy. He felt ill but there was no time to think about it, for at that moment there was the clatter of a helicopter in the sky above the houses.

"Modimo!" Mama Dora exclaimed as she came out of the bedroom, the buttons of her dress still unfastened. "Get away from that window, Mannetjie! Why are you fooling around with your head out of the window? Do you want them to start shooting, hey?"

She shouldn't have said that. Maria gave one long wail and jumped at her mother, almost knocking her over. Her arms and legs opened at the same time: she looked like a frog jumping into the water. As she grabbed Ma, there was a sound of tearing and Ma's dress gaped in front.

"Now, just look what the child—" Mama Dora scolded. But suddenly she stopped because, somewhere, a great many voices began shouting and singing. They were young voices—the sound came from the direction of the school.

"If I could move away from here, I'd go," said Mama Dora emphatically. Her face was ashen. Adam looked at her, and suddenly it came to him what she looked like; Ntate's face had looked like that when they took him out from under the threshing machine.

"I'm scared, Ma," Maria cried, and Evon chimed in: "Scared! Scared!"

"We're all scared," Mama Dora said suddenly. "Satan is loose in this place."

Mama Dora knew three devils: the ordinary imp who made children wilful and disobedient, the devil who made her believe that Uncle Saul would be killed in the mine at Welkom, and Satan. Against Satan you were powerless: he could kill and make people disappear so that you never saw them again. One of Mama Dora's neighbors had disappeared like that. Her sons had found her shoes and her headcloth in the underpass, but she never came home again. People said that Satan had been in the underpass that night.

"I'm going to see," said Sefanya. He buttoned his shirt hurriedly, his eyes wild.

"You don't put a foot outside that door," snapped Mama Dora, grabbing him by the shoulder. "You move one step out of here and I'll . . . I'll whip you!" She walked to the door to see if it was on the latch; the screws were so loose that the door could be opened if you just pushed against it from the outside, even if it was on the latch.

"You must cut small pieces of wood," said Mama Dora, "so that we can push them into the screw holes. The latch won't hold if the holes are so big,"

"It's Sefanya who did such bad work," said Moses sullenly. "He was the last one to fill the holes, Mama. But he does everything by half."

Ma and Mama Dora weren't really listening to him. Their heads were cocked, their eyes narrowed, as they tried to hear what was going on outside. The noise of the helicopter was louder again: its clatter drowned all other sounds. Suddenly, there was a loud noise; the walls felt as though they were shaking. Adam could have sworn that the crack above the back door was widening. The helicopter sounded farther away.

"What was that?" Ma whispered.

Somewhere near the school, there was the sound of a shot, and then another. The helicopter was circling, and the clatter was louder again.

"Only Modimo can help us today," said Mama Dora.

But after the shots and the shouting, it was suddenly

quiet. Something banged softly against the back door and the bantams cackled. Chased by the cock, the little hen had flown against the door.

The worst was surely over. The bantam cock was as clever as a dog — if he'd chased the hen, then surely there couldn't be any danger near the house.

Adam's nose was running and he wiped it with the back of his hand. Pain throbbed behind his eyes.

They ate bread in strict silence. Mama Dora was intent on listening to what was going on outside. The more Sefanya nagged at her, the angrier she became.

"Perhaps I should go and see if there are any children at school," he said trying to look as innocent as he could.

"You stay right here," said Mama Dora. "Listen to me, Sefanya! If you go out of that door I'll let your father know at the mine. How can I stop something happening to you if you won't listen?"

"I won't go near any people!" Sefanya said sullenly. "Everybody knows what's going on, Mama. Only we have to sit at home, dying of boredom."

"Then you can die of boredom in the house," said Mama Dora in her church voice. "Outside in the streets you'll die from a shot." She looked at Ma as though asking for help. "This child gives me headaches. If I'd gone to work today, what would've happened? You'd have slept in the cells tonight, Sefanya. *Mosadi*, it's not easy to raise children!"

"Must we stay in the house for the whole day, Mama Dora?" Magdalene asked. She was lisping and it suddenly seemed to Adam as if her loose tooth was hanging by a thread, swinging to and fro. "The whole, whole day?"

"When I'm sure that everything is quiet," said Mama Dora, "you can sit in the backyard. But only in the backyard. If I find one of you in the street — only one — you'll all clean floors."

They ate bread and syrup and it was as quiet as if there were an illness in the house. No one spoke, no one nudged anybody else or laughed. Only Magdalene made sounds with her tongue against her gums. Adam listened: he could hear her breath whistling through the gap between her tooth and gum.

"Pull the stupid thing!" said Paul the Pest, reaching toward her. She knocked his hand away, her eyes as round as marbles.

"Do you want my tooth to bleed?" she asked indignantly.

"*Mosadi!*" said Mama Dora. "When you children are so naughty, I want to take my smock and go to work, even if those people on the road do grab me!"

To keep them out of mischief, she gave them work to do. They had to scour the pots with steel wool and soap until they shone like mirrors. They had to clean the legs of the chairs and break the dry branches on the woodpile into small pieces. Sefanya and Moses had to fix the rickety latch; they did so, muttering and complaining. Adam and Edward had to wash the diapers.

"But it's woman's work!" said Edward indignantly.

"There is no such thing as woman's work and man's work anymore," said Mama Dora, and her voice sounded like the rams' horns of Gideon in the Bible. "With work I'll keep you and the police out of each other's way." She saw Mannetjie on the sagging wire fence. "Mannetjie! Get away from there! There's nothing for you on the street. Come and peel the potatoes."

They worked, but all day long they heard the sounds: the droning of Casspirs and police vans, voices shouting, what sounded like gunshots. A few times, people ran past, and once, the helicopter circled low over the houses. "Attention, attention," a booming voice shouted over the bullhorn in the helicopter. "Please go back to your homes. You'll be hurt if you don't go to your homes."

Evon cried because of the helicopter. Maria hid under the table, and even Edward was ashen-faced.

"How long will it last, Ma?" Edward asked.

"Not long," she replied, continuing to look outside. "Just stay here; it won't last long. Tomorrow everything will be fine again." But Adam heard her whispering: "Modimo! Modimo!"

That evening Ma and Mama Dora made them stand around the table. Mama Dora prayed first: that the Lord would be with them during the night, that he would care for them as a hen cares for her chicks — that the wings of the Lord would shelter them.

Every morning that week, when Adam was woken by the twins crying in the bedroom, he knew: Modimo's wings *had* sheltered them. But Modimo still hadn't made the street quiet. Outside there was the crack of police whips, and the sound of people throwing stones. In the streets all hell had been let loose. And Adam's head and throat were still aching.

Sefanya kept creeping out from under Modimo's wings; every now and then he disappeared, and Mama Dora would look as though she'd seen a corpse. But when he came back, Mama Dora couldn't whip him because he was bigger than she was — he was as big as Uncle Saul.

"The coffee's finished," said Mama Dora on Thursday morning. "You children must ask before you make coffee. You know we can't go to work or buy what we want."

"They made one woman drink all the paraffin she'd bought," said Moses suddenly. "Truly."

"Who made her drink it?" Edward asked.

"The people who wait along the road, of course!"

"There's very little mealie meal left," said Mama Dora, ignoring the boys. "And hardly any sugar."

Adam saw his mother's face. Her eyes looked very,

very old. She stood, with Jacob in a blanket on her back and Esau half over her shoulder; he cried all day because he had colic. Ma had grown smaller, he thought. Like Magdalene's Kgatwane. Perhaps Ma was also getting smaller because she cried so much. He knew that she cried quietly, when she thought no one saw her. The coffee, sugar, and mealie meal were all things Ma had helped Mama Dora buy. When they were finished, Mama Dora wouldn't be kind to Ma any longer.

He looked again at Ma, noting that her eyes looked like the broken lens of old Hansie's glasses. Suddenly he wished he could touch her. But you didn't touch your mother; you didn't touch women. He watched her rubbing Esau's back with her work-hardened hand and thought: I must think of a plan fast. I'll just have to go to work on Saturday! I'm not *moshemane* — a boy — any longer; if Ntate were here he would also have said that I must be called *monna* — a man.

He felt his throat tighten. How will I get back with the newspaper money? he wondered. I didn't think of that. How will I get back with the money? It's going to be hard enough leaving here with stones flying and broken bottles everywhere, and smoke hanging over the township . . .

He shivered as he watched Esau's angry little arms finally relax in tiredness and sleep. If they catch me, he thought. . . . He wished he could run away from his own thoughts like a cat running from a strange smell on its own patch. If they catch me, they'll set Mama Dora's house on fire. There was more than enough smoke outside — as well as a terrible smell — as though everything were burning at once: blankets, plastic, hair, bodies, houses. The fires that were burning outside knew no mercy.

chapter 7

On Friday morning Adam was woken by some-
one hitting him in the stomach. He felt cold with fright.
But it was only Magdalene, crouching beside him and
trying to push something into one of his eyes. "I told
you!" she said, her fingers touching his eyelids.
"Look!"

He pushed her arm away and tried to blink the sleep
from his eyes.

"But it's the middle of the night, Magdalene!"

"It's out!" she said and something small slid down
his neck. "Now you've lost it! Don't move!"

"Is it your tooth?" asked Adam, remembering his
sister's obsession. He felt among the blankets and
found it. "There you are."

"You're not even pleased," she said accusingly. She
grabbed the tooth and looked at him haughtily. "Tonight Kgatwane will come and then you'll be sorry!"

Adam's stomach tightened into a knot. Why did girls
have to be so silly? Why did that big-mouth Agnes
have to tell Magdalene such stories?

"Listen, Magdalene," he said, thinking fast. "Kgatwane won't come tonight. He only comes when — when it's safe. There are too many Casspirs in the streets now. He'll get run over. Keep that tooth and when — "

But the little girl pouted, her eyes full of tears. "Will he . . . never come again?"

"Who — Kgatwane? Of course he'll come again! He's only scared of the noise now."

She rubbed the tooth between her fingers, her face wet with tears. "Then Kgatwane is like a bird," she said, sniffing.

"Why is Kgatwane like a bird?" asked Adam and saw, from the corner of his eye, Evon turning in her sleep and feeling for the torn and tickling corner of her blanket.

"A bird," said Magdalene gravely, "only stays where it's quiet. That's why there are no birds here. Now, you tell me Kgatwane is also scared of noise. So Kgatwane is just like a bird."

For a brief moment Adam remembered the birds at the power station. They lived in the noise of the city and it didn't seem to bother them. His thoughts jumped to the newspaper bird which had flown away from him and old Hansie, in amongst the cars. That bird was used to noise: stamped with black printer's ink, the cars hooting, and old Labuschagne's bleating. But that bird is not alive, Adam! he reminded himself.

"I'm just waiting for those Casspirs to stop making a noise and then I'll put out my tooth for Kgatwane. There's no point in telling me he'll never come."

"He'll come," agreed Adam in a tired voice. "You'll see." But immediately he felt like kicking himself for making such a stupid promise.

That day, Mama Dora made him clean the floors, but during the afternoon Adam knew he had to speak to his mother. The supply of coffee was finished; there weren't enough diapers; the twins woke up every few minutes. Ma was growing smaller and smaller from crying on her own and not eating enough. The time to speak to her had come.

But just as he wanted to talk to her, fighting broke out in the backyard. Adam sat with the floor cloth in his hands, listening.

Mama Dora lost her temper on the spot. "*Mosadi*," she exclaimed to Ma. "Today those children are looking for trouble!" She yanked open the back door and, through it, Adam saw Paul and Mannetjie, Magdalene, Edward, and Maria, standing to attention, like soldiers.

They stamped their feet and lifted their clenched fists above their heads. He heard them shouting, "Away with school! Away with books!" Somebody was yelling loudly enough to make the windowpanes rattle, and as Adam got up he saw Sefanya hitting Moses across the legs with a piece of rope tied to a stick. Sefanya was laughing as though they were playing a game, but something was clearly very wrong.

Mama Dora threw down the dishcloth she was holding and stormed outside, her dress streaming behind her. She grabbed Sefanya by the shoulder, although he was as tall as Uncle Saul, and held his arm so that the stick remained aloft like a flagpole.

"Sefanya!" she shouted. "Have you no sense? What do you think you're doing?"

"It's a game," said Sefanya sulkily. "There's nothing to do, so we're playing a game!" But it was obvious from Sefanya's voice that he was not telling the truth.

"It's not a game," said Mama Dora furiously, her face ashen. "You're playing pretend games while your mothers have to go to work. . . . We have to get up early in the morning and go to bed when the night is old so that you can go to school. Don't you dare play those games at my house again. You stay out of things you don't understand, do you hear me?"

Adam washed the floor cloth and hung it over the wire fence. He saw Sefanya and Moses sitting against the wall of the house, far from each other, while Evon crawled on the ground, her dress getting more and more dirty.

I don't want to live here anymore, he thought, looking across scruffy backyards. I'm tired of everything. But almost all the tins of food are empty. Mama Dora is getting more and more short-tempered and there is nothing Ma can do. If I don't do something very soon, we won't even have a roof over our heads.

Ma was busy tidying the room as he closed the door behind him. He heard one of the twins making little sucking noises, as though he were dreaming of milk.

"Ma," he said softly, "I've been thinking. I won't stay away from work. I'll leave this afternoon so that no one knows I'm going to work, and I'll sleep in the city tonight. Tomorrow, and on Sunday, I'll sell newspapers, and I'll come home on Sunday afternoon. They won't be on the road on a Sunday afternoon, Ma."

Ma froze. "No, Adam, you can't go to work," she said.

Was it possible that she knew how scared he was? Adam wondered. That she knew about the houses being burned down? He had tried to make it all sound so easy. . . .

"It's a lot of money, Ma," he said. "If I don't go, everything will be used up: sugar, meal — everything. This time you must let me go. I'm not small anymore — I'm taking Ntate's place. I'll be careful . . . I'll ask Modimo to help me."

"You're only a child," said Ma desperately.

"But I'm nearly a man," Adam replied.

"I don't want to lose you," she said and looked outside. She stood like that for a long time, her head turned away from him. When she spoke to him again, she wiped a finger over her eyes as though flicking away dust. "If I lose you," she said, "I'll lose all hope."

"It won't happen," he said. "I'll go to work and, you'll see — I'll bring home money. I'll pray, Ma."

She didn't forbid him to go in the end, but when the others complained that they were hungry and Mama Dora gave them the previous day's vetkoek and tea, Adam was given two helpings. "You must keep one for this evening, Adam," Ma said. "Where are you going to sleep?"

"At the newspaper," he said. As though old Labuschagne would allow him to sleep there!

"Are other children going to sleep there as well?" his mother asked, sounding a little less anxious.

"I suppose so, Ma. Some of the others said they wouldn't stay away either." He knew he was lying, but her face looked so old and unhappy that he just couldn't tell her the truth.

"Then you must take blankets," said Ma. "So that you won't be cold. Don't think I haven't heard you sniffing the past few days."

He had to think fast. "They steal your blankets," he said on the spur of the moment. "I'll dress warmly, Ma. I'll be fine like that."

Sefanya, Edward, and Paul the Pest stared at him, open-mouthed. "If they catch you, they'll burn the house down," said Sefanya. "I think you're mad."

"I don't have a father any longer," said Adam and

felt himself flushing. "My mother can't go to work while she's feeding the babies. Where will the money come from if one of us doesn't go out to work?"

"They'll catch you, sure as anything," said Paul the Pest, his mouth full of vetkoek.

"You must take the bicycle wheel with you," said Edward out of the blue. "And a stick to roll it. If it looks as if you're playing, they won't grab you."

Adam recognized it as being a good idea. He went to fetch the old bicycle wheel and the stick in the backyard, and suddenly he felt full of courage. I must run along pretending to play, he thought. With a bicycle wheel I can just trot past them — it won't look as if I'm going to work.

Jacob was at his mother's breast when Adam went to say goodbye. He smelled baby blankets and soap and petroleum jelly, and saw how rounded Jacob's little arms had become. All his wrinkles were gone. So, he thought, the children are getting fat and Ma is shrinking.

"I'll just say *sala hantle* — stay well, Ma," he said, his throat closing.

She looked up slowly and her eyes were very dark. "*Tsamaya hantle* — go well, Adam," she said. "You must come back, my son."

He closed the door again, grabbed the stick and the wheel and left by the front door without saying goodbye to anyone else. The wheel reflected the strong sunlight.

Adam's eyes were full of tears and his nose was running. It was only when the wheel fell over for the first time that he remembered what he was supposed to be doing.

The streets were full of children; it looked like holiday time. The small ones were wrestling and shouting and crawling on hands and knees while the older ones leaned against walls and fences and parked cars. It was impossible to tell friend from foe. There were no Casspirs in sight; at first glance everything was as usual.

Except, Adam realized, Samuel wasn't there. His father had kept him at home because he didn't think that what was happening in Phameng was safe for children. If Samuel wasn't allowed out, then something really was wrong.

Adam spun the wheel and steered it across the open veld with the stick. Sing, Adam, he told himself. Sing, so that they can't know what's in your heart. He jogged along behind the wheel, unable to think of any song to sing. He'd forgotten every song he knew. It was from fear, he knew. Sing, Adam! And he started his own song: "*Dumela, ausi . . . dumela, nkgono . . . wena o kae . . . wena o kae . . .* how are you . . ."

Then suddenly, probably because he wished that Samuel was running next to him, he sang, "The name of my friend is Sa-mu-hel . . . Sa-mu-hel . . . The name of my friend is . . ."

He steered the wheel across the veld, recalling the

story of Lot when Sodom and Gomorrah were burning behind him. You're done for if you look back, Lot, the angel had said. One glance and you'll be changed into a pillar of salt, so hard and rough that the cattle will use you as a lick.

I must not look back, Adam thought, and he could have sworn that he heard broken glass crackling behind him. First he was hot, then cold, then hot again and cold. The wheel started to wobble, then stopped after giving a final hop, skip, and jump over the grass tufts. When he bent down, he peered between his legs. Behind him was an upside-down world. Sodom and Gomorrah must have seemed like this to Lot and his wife.

The Lord had sent fire and sulfur from heaven, he thought, and reached for the wheel. He missed it, and a duwweltjie stuck in his finger. He straightened and sucked at his finger to ease the burning. His legs were shaking. If he hadn't seen the duwweltjie with his own eyes, he would have been convinced a poisonous snake had bitten him because he wanted to get out of Phameng.

Sodom and Gomorrah had probably been like Phameng, he thought. His finger hurt so much that he had to keep sucking it. When he did finally look back, he could see only black walls, ash, and multicolored smoke.

He bent down to pick up the wheel, and started

pushing it past the rubbish heap on his right. His finger ached painfully from the duwweltjie's poison. He was sure his shadow was making a noise as it moved along from grass tuft to grass tuft, behind him.

"I'm not scared," he said to give himself courage. "Why should I be scared?"

"You're so scared you could wet yourself," said another voice in his head. "No, look ahead! Looking back doesn't help. It's your shadow that frightens you. When you're alone, your shadow rustles like that."

"I'm not scared. I mustn't look as though I'm in a hurry. If someone is watching me, it must seem as though I'm playing with the wheel. If someone is watching me, I must make him tired of watching, just as I get tired of watching Evangedi in Sunday school. The watcher must start thinking of something else, the way I so often do when Evangedi is speaking about sin."

"You're so scared you could wet yourself."

"I'm not scared. There's no one behind me — it is only the wind rustling in the grass."

Adam hadn't noticed the big boy lying against the slope of the rubbish heap, and when he heard his voice right in front of him, his body jerked with fright and his legs turned to water.

"Where are you going?"

The wheel wobbled and ran into a stone. The sound rang through his head.

"Me . . . ? Nowhere," Adam replied in a hoarse voice.

"What are you doing here, so far from home?" The boy raised himself slightly. His skin was pitted, and things that looked like medals were pinned to his vest. His arms were like steel pipes covered with ash from the rubbish heap.

"I'm spinning . . . my wheel," Adam stuttered. "I'm playing."

The big boy crooked a finger. "Come here."

"What?" Adam's lips were as dry as his throat.

"Come here, stupid!"

Adam looked over his shoulder and felt his stomach do a flip. But he had no choice; he had to go nearer.

"Bend down," said the big boy, still sitting. Adam crouched down. He could see the cracks in the boy's scaly knees. The hands grabbing at his gray school shirt were lightly scarred.

The big boy grabbed the pocket of his shirt and rummaged through it. "Why are you wearing your school shirt, hey?"

"I don't . . . have any other clothes," Adam whispered. The hands moved over his body and it felt as though a python were slithering toward his pockets. Adam froze, waiting for orders from the bigger boy. The hands stopped their rummaging. "What do you have in your trouser pocket, hey?"

In his trouser pocket? He couldn't think for a moment. But eventually his mind started working again, perhaps because he caught the oily smell of the vetkoek on the changing wind.

"Oh, that!" he said, swallowing hard, his legs weak. "That's only . . . my vetkoek."

The bigger boy leaned against the bank of the rubbish heap, shifting his shoulders until he was comfortable. Adam could see the palm of the hand approaching; he could see every line on it.

"Hand over, stupid," said the bigger boy. "Why are you standing there like a dead sheep?"

"M-must I give . . . the vetkoek?"

The boy spat violently at Adam's face. "Are you handing it over, or aren't you?"

Adam pulled the vetkoek from his pocket and saw that it was covered with threads. Nervously, he tried to wipe the threads off the vetkoek.

"Damn it, give!" the bigger boy suddenly shouted. "And get away from here . . . move it! Go and tell your mother that when she makes me vetkoek again she must wrap it in newspaper, d'you hear?"

Should I pick up the wheel and keep running toward the city? Adam wondered. The boy was one of *them*. . . . I can't openly run toward the tarred road while he lies against the rubbish dump watching me, can I?

His hands were trembling as he picked up the stick and pressed the point into the groove of the wheel.

Perhaps I should turn back. It's not going to work.

They're going to burn down Mama Dora's house, with Ma and the babies and everyone else in it. I can't. I can't go on.

He stumbled over the tufts of dried grass. Broken glass glittered in the afternoon sun. I must not look back, not once. If I keep going toward the tarred road, he must not see me looking back — he'll come after me.

Slowly, his mind started working again. I've never seen that boy before, he thought. He's not in the blue-roof school. He's never seen me before, either. He doesn't know where I live. He can't get up from the rubbish dump to go and burn down Mama Dora's house because he doesn't know I live there.

His breath whistled, and there was a burning in his throat when he swallowed. I must not look back, Adam thought. If I were to start running close to the tarred road . . . If I could only reach the opposite side, with the cars coming from the front and the buses and things between me and the boy . . .

Once I'm on the tarred road I can start running. He won't be able to catch me.

Adam had to clench his teeth to stop himself looking back. He thought he could hear clods of earth breaking behind him. He ran past some cattle; they raised their big heads to watch him. He smelled them, smelled his own fear. But the black line of the tarred road stretched straight ahead with the cars roaring past. He swallowed a few times and steered the wheel over the last bit of veld.

With a jump and a grinding of metal the wheel hit the tarred road to the city.

When he was in Mama Dora's house in Phameng and he thought about the city, he had imagined that there were lots of empty plots and half-built cluster houses where he could sleep at night. But five kilometers is a long way to roll a wheel; it gave him enough time to worry about what he was going to do when he got there.

In the city he suddenly saw how many people there were on the earth. No matter where he looked, there were people. The streets looked like ant trails. When he tired of walking, he could stand still and just sniff: the smell of popcorn and doughnuts, of coffee wafting from the coffee shops; he could even smell the tomatoes that the old tomato seller in Maitland Street was offering to passersby. Some of the children were eating chocolate ice cream, others chewing gum. Adam felt like an idiot clutching the stupid wheel under his arm.

He was startled when he saw the orange safety jacket with the word *Focus* on it in front of him. A white boy, new to the job and overeager, was selling newspapers. "Newspaper, sir?" he asked politely. "Newspaper, lady?"

It's one of the boys from the Children's Home, Adam thought miserably, coming to a halt. Here was one of the children from the Children's Home on the beat already!

The boy clearly knew nothing about selling newspapers. He covered the headlines with his hands and tried to run to cars when the traffic lights were green. Neither did he have his change ready: he dug into his pockets while the buyers frowned, holding out their hands.

They won't take my place tomorrow, Adam thought. I'll keep my job even if I have to sleep in a park tonight. And suddenly he knew where he was going to sleep.

The day, several months ago, the standard-five children were taken to the National Museum, they had all had to wait for a while on the lawns of Hertzog Square. A schoolteacher had gone to ask if they could go inside, and while she was away, they sat on the lawn, eating oranges.

The wind had been blowing and the fine spray from the fountains made them feel fresh after the sweatiness of the bus. There were statues and terraces and flowers and a long row of fountains — it was a nice place in which to wait. Adam had noticed a couple of tramps lying under the stairs. So, there is enough space to lie down under the stairs, Adam thought, relieved. If only the tramps hadn't got there first!

He started walking in the direction of the square. Why am I so hungry? he wondered. I had something to eat this afternoon. But he knew it was because the big boy had taken the other vetkoek. The moment you know there's no water, your throat becomes dry. The moment you know your vetkoek is gone, your stomach starts rumbling. He could see the boy's bad skin again, and it was almost as though he heard the lazy voice near him. I mustn't think about that now, he thought. They'll see it on my face. Nothing must show on my face. But he kept on shivering. He was cold and hot at the same time. He walked up Maitland Street and started counting the hours on his fingers: sixteen hours to Saturday morning at eight when the newspaper sales could start; twenty hours before he would have money to buy food.

There had to be food somewhere. Even the tramps stayed alive. You didn't see people dying of hunger on the streets; somehow everyone found something to eat. Or were there many people around whose stomachs cried with hunger the way Evon cried from earache?

Four o'clock. Twenty hours was too long. Nobody could wait for *twenty hours* for a stupid piece of bread and a slice of polony. Ntate always said you should never allow yourself to be reduced to pulp. Modimo has given you two hands, two feet and one head, Ntate always said. With that you can look after yourself. You didn't have to be ground down.

Adam stood still. Modimo! he thought. What am I going to do with two hands, two feet, and one head if the boys from the Children's Home are already out there with the newspapers? Where can I find a new job

94

at this time of day, especially when my head feels as though it's filled with water?

It flashed through his mind that with his hands he could dig and rake and do other things. Perhaps he could push the carts at one of the big stores — Samuel had said that the store at the high apartment building stayed open until six.

He clutched the wheel uncomfortably under his arm and started running. It was far to go — and it felt as though he was standing still. The wheel cut into his arm and he wished he could get rid of it, but he would never hear the end of it from Edward, who played with it every day. It was stupid to have dragged the wheel along.

There were many cars in the parking area in front of the store; people were probably shopping after work. He looked around and saw the security guard in front of the video shop, next to the main entrance. Why am I scared? Adam wondered. I'm not stealing anything, I'm simply asking if I can push someone's cart. I'll put the wheel against the wall. If it disappears, it disappears.

He saw an old lady approaching with her cart, swallowed, and gathered together the little bit of courage he had.

"Excuse me, madam, may I push the cart, please, madam?"

If she had said "No, thank you," he would almost certainly have run away, leaving the wheel against the wall. But she looked at his face as if to see whether he were honest, and he saw her hands leaving the handle of the cart even before she said: "Thank you very much — it's the little yellow car in front of the dry cleaners. But be careful with the eggs."

He earned just enough money in tips to buy half a loaf of bread and a half liter of milk, but it was better than nothing. While he was buying the food he felt quite lightheaded with pleasure: he had managed to look after himself! But when he was out on the street again, he shivered involuntarily. The dark came so early, and with the dark the dampness of winter. Everything became damp: the walls, the cement on the pavements, the grass. Every few minutes he had to wipe his runny nose on the back of his hand.

Was the big boy still standing guard at the rubbish dump? Adam asked himself. Or had he found out where Mama Dora's house was? He clenched his teeth. I mustn't think about that. . . . It's no use being worried — I can't do anything from where I am. I've come as far as this, there's no going back now. I'll stay here, in the light of the café, he thought, his feet suddenly reluctant to walk to the square. As long as he sat in the light, it seemed warmer. And his head felt better. It was best to try to forget about the rubbish dump and the hard eyes of the big boy.

He knew he was being foolish and that he shouldn't delay going to the park. He couldn't go groping around in the dark under the stairs to find out if there was room to sleep — he might stick his fingers into a tramp's eye!

Adam sighed and picked up the wheel. I can't go back to Phameng, he realized, and felt his body becoming icy cold. I've burned my boats. I was crazy to come, but I'm here now, and I'll just have to carry on.

It was almost dark when he reached the square. The fountains were noisy and he could smell the water. The grass already smelled of night. But there were also other unpleasant smells: dogs and people must have made messes under the bushes and against the walls.

Adam felt like a thief as he peered under the stairs. He waited with bated breath, for his eyes had to get used to the shadows. Nothing moved, and in the half-light he recognized objects: an old shoe, beer cans. He squatted, then started to gather the beer cans. Suddenly, he wanted to cry. I don't want to sleep here! he wanted to shout.

But there was nothing he could do. He knew of no other place to hide in the city that night. There was nothing for it but to sleep under the stairs.

Feeling his way slowly, he crept under the stairs. The smell of tramps became stronger. What if those people come back tonight? he thought. He banged his head and saw stars, and for a few moments he was too dizzy to think at all.

There was no other way. He curled up and closed

his eyes. Modimo, he thought. Modimo — tonight I'm asking nicely that Modimo must please keep those wings over me!

But Modimo felt very far away. Ntate always said the Lord was like a shepherd: if you closed your eyes, you could see him with his shepherd's crook. Just as a shepherd always heard when one of his sheep was caught in a thorn bush, so Modimo heard when you called. You simply had to close your eyes and believe, and Modimo would hear you.

For once Ntate hadn't told the truth. I can only see Samuel's face when I close my eyes, Adam thought. There's no sign of a shepherd's crook — all I can see are Samuel's jaws moving as he chews gum. All I see is Samuel's narrow face, and his careful eyes.

Well then, what did I say? Adam thought, and it felt as though he were speaking to Samuel. I told you. You can get past the troublemakers. I managed it.

Tiredness must have confused him, because it sounded exactly as though Samuel were speaking to him: *I still think you're crazy. It's not coming here; it's going back that's difficult.*

Be cozy under your blankets, Samuel! Adam thought, and suddenly he was furious with his friend. Sleep well, with your stomach full of food, the doors and windows shut against the cold.

Then he felt ashamed. It wasn't Samuel's fault. It

wasn't Samuel who had told him to spend the night here.

He lay there, his body aching, but he couldn't sleep. Late at night he heard people walking up and down the stairs. In the darkness a man and a woman spoke to each other, close by; the girl laughed and then there was silence. He didn't hear them walking away; he knew they were still sitting on the stairs above him. He didn't dare move. Suppose they heard him and hauled him out?

Later, a long time after he'd first heard them, the man suddenly said loudly: "We'll have to go. Look how high the moon is!" Only after that was the square completely silent.

If the moon showed that the night was already old, surely the tramps must've found another place to sleep. If you were tired and hungry, you didn't go looking for shelter at this time of night.

It was only then, when he was almost sure that the tramps wouldn't return to the place under the stairs, that Adam straightened his cramped legs and dozed off.

All night long the cold kept on waking him. He tried everything: a few times he even knelt, his arms folded round his body, but the cold sliced through his clothes.

By the early hours of the morning the cold had confused him: he kept fumbling, thinking his blankets had shifted. While he was feeling around for his blankets, he touched something that felt like paper. Instantly, he was wide awake. There was a pile of newspapers at the far end of his hiding place.

If it had been daylight, he would certainly have checked to see whether there were spiders or other insects in that pile, but he was too cold and too confused to think of things like that. He fumbled with stiff fingers until the papers opened and by the time he fell asleep again, exhausted, a few pieces of newspaper were wrapped around the coldest parts of his body.

When the daylight came, he remained where he was, because there was nothing else to do. His body hurt and he was coughing — the cold must have affected his throat. His clothes were as damp as the newspapers with which he'd covered himself; he felt like a discarded piece of rubbish.

Suddenly, he heard a dog barking, close to the stairs. His body stiffened as he heard the sound of the dog's paws on the gravel path next to the stairs. Before he could gather his thoughts, the dog was in front of him, growling. The police! Adam thought. He felt his body go numb. He couldn't move; indeed, he could hardly breathe. Only his stomach wasn't dead. His stomach contracted around the previous evening's half-loaf and he felt like vomiting.

"Rex!" came a man's voice, and Adam saw the dog straining against the lead. "Come on, Rex!"

100

Two legs appeared behind the dog — old legs with slippered feet. The dog barked furiously, scrabbling in the loose gravel, digging in.

"What's the matter with you?" the old man's voice asked. He bent down and a round face peered in under the stairs. "It's just a lot of old papers," said the old man, but the words hung in the air. "But — hey! What are you doing down there, *umfana?*"

Umfana? Umfana? Then it was safe. The old man had said it quietly. He hadn't spoken as people would speak to a bit of rubbish. Son, he'd said. Son . . . son . . . but in Zulu.

Adam tried to get up, but the stairs were too low and the dog too close.

"The dog . . ." he said.

The old man dragged the dog away and Adam crawled out. Bits of dried grass and gravel were clinging to him and he had a dirty taste in his mouth, as though there were damp soil between his teeth.

"Are you hiding?" the old man asked above the barking of the dog.

"No, master," said Adam, wishing that he could stop coughing. "I only came to work, master."

"You're not allowed to sleep here," said the old man. "What is the square going to look like if everyone sleeps here? I won't report you, but if I were you I'd find myself another place to sleep. Don't you have a mother and a father?"

"I have a mother," Adam said softly.

"Then you don't have to sleep here," said the old man. "Rex! Sit!"

The dog sat, but kept showing its teeth. Adam shivered with cold. He was a bit lightheaded and had to hold on to the railing next to him not to fall over.

"I suppose you've run away from home," the old man said suddenly. "If I may give you good advice, go home today. The world is too cruel for boys like you. Go back to your mother and tell her you're sorry — and become the kind of young man of whom she can be proud one day. You don't belong under the stairs."

Then the old man took his dog and walked away.

As soon as he was out of sight, Adam crept under the stairs again. He could hardly believe it, but it was true: after standing in the cold he realized it was warmer in the damp, moldy shelter of the stairs. He pulled his knees under his chin, wrapped his arms round his body, and fell asleep again.

chapter 8

Old Labuschagne was already in his cubicle and calling out names when Adam arrived. The place seemed unfamiliar to Adam because there were so many youngsters from the Children's Home. But Willem Maerman, sliding the piles of newspapers along the counter as usual, looked up and his jaw dropped. "And that one, master?" he said, jerking his head in Adam's direction. "Where does that one come from?"

Old Labuschagne turned his face, but all you could see were his moustache and glasses. "Oh," he said. "So you've turned up, after all."

"Catch!" Willem Maerman said and shot Parkway's newspapers to Adam over the counter.

Suddenly everything seemed the same as usual: old Hansie struggling to get into the minibus, Taffie Venter scratching scabs off his legs, Willem Maerman running in and out of cafés. The Children's Home lot sat there like old hands—as though they were going to sell papers forever.

The corner at the Parkway Police Station was so busy that there was no time to do sums. You handed over change like a money machine. Old Hansie was slow — time after time, when the lights changed, he was still standing next to a car, desperately searching for the right coins. Then a blast of honking would burst out behind him because the long row of cars couldn't pass. The noise sliced through Adam's head: he felt as though he had to narrow his eyes to stop the blaring tunneling into his brain. He had difficulty staying upright. He felt as if he had just got out of bed after having had a runny tummy for a long time. And every time he coughed, his head hurt.

"Why do you look like that?" asked old Hansie, while they waited for the stream of traffic to pass. "I've been watching you holding your head. Are you sleeping badly with the new babies in the house?"

"My head has been thick all week," said Adam. "But it's hurting on both sides today." He was almost too tired to speak. "When the cars make so much noise, it feels as though a train is going over my head. And when I cough, it feels like someone is knocking a nail into my head from the inside."

"But you must be ill, Adam, boy," said old Hansie as they slipped across the street. The cars roared past them and, one after another, came to a halt. The piles of newspapers became smaller, the sun became whiter and warmer, but not warm enough to banish the goose pimples from Adam's body.

104

Ill? Adam thought. How can I be ill now, when Ma and the others are waiting for me in Mama Dora's house? I've come to the city to sell newspapers, not to be ill.

"Does your mother know that you're coughing like this?" old Hansie wanted to know. "Doesn't she give you cough medicine? You're going to cough yourself into the grave."

"I'll only see my mother again tomorrow afternoon," said Adam.

Old Hansie's head twitched as though he didn't understand. "Why only then?"

"I can't get home," Adam said. "Look — it's in the newspaper: everything's gone wrong in Phameng."

"Where are you sleeping?" asked old Hansie with a frown.

But then the lights changed to red and people honked for newspapers. The fifth car in the row was a small red one, the man and woman in it sitting as close together as Dr. Marx's rabbits did when they were cold. Willem Maerman said that when two people sat like that, you knew they weren't married. You could just as well give them the wrong change; they wouldn't even bother to look. But the man paid with a five-rand note; you couldn't treat that like a fifty-cent piece. Adam scrabbled in his pocket; goose pimples covered his body and he was lightheaded. He couldn't do sums anymore. He tried to count out the change in his hand.

"Don't bother," said the man and looked at the

woman as though she was the prettiest thing in the world.

"But it's — " Adam began. Then the light changed to green and the small car shot away. Adam, his mouth hanging open, stood with the money in his hand. It couldn't be true. Five rands!

"He just drove away," he said to old Hansie, who had seen it happen.

"It's your jackpot today," said old Hansie. "Probably wanted to show the girl that he's rolling in money. Some people are like that. But tell me now: where are you sleeping tonight?"

Adam turned over the five-rand note to see whether it was real. "In the . . ." he began, but he couldn't bear to say "the park." "I'll find a place," he said lamely.

"What kind of place?" old Hansie asked. "Adam, where did you sleep last night?"

Adam looked up and everything seemed to be spinning slightly, as though he'd been on the turnabout at the park in the zoo. I'm too ill to open my mouth, he thought. I've got a purple note in my hand and I'm not even happy about it. I can't think properly because the cold is gripping my scalp and neck.

"Where, hey?"

"Near here," said Adam and his voice sounded far away, as though he were dreaming. "Under the stairs on Hertzog Square."

106

"In this cold?" old Hansie asked. "Are you mad? That's why you're coughing like that, man!"

"Where else can I sleep?" Adam asked, watching the traffic light. He was too tired to explain; he wished he could lie down.

But Hansie's voice came out of the gray mist around him. "I can give you somewhere to doss down. It's hard but at least you'll have a roof over your head."

"Where . . . ?" Adam stuttered.

"You'll die in this cold," said old Hansie. "Tonight you can sleep in my room."

"Are you going home?" old Hansie asked Taffie Venter. They had paid their money in, and old Hansie seemed to be in a great hurry.

Taffie pulled a scab off his leg and blotted the watery blood with his finger. "I'm staying right here," he said. "You can tell my mother that I've still got work to do at the newspaper."

Adam tried to listen, but his head was too muzzy to make any sense of what they were saying.

"I was just thinking," said old Hansie. "Adam isn't feeling well; he keeps on coughing. So I thought . . . if you were going home, Adam could lie down there for the afternoon. I can't let him stay there alone. There are pills in the room as well."

"I remember, you're going to the war thing this afternoon," said Taffie. He glanced at Adam and stuck out his lower lip. "I can take him, okay, but I'm not staying in that place tonight. I'll show him where everything is, then I'm going off again."

"Here's the key," said old Hansie. "You know where the box of medicine is. Give him some of the cough syrup and put down the gray blanket for him."

"Aren't you going home at all?" Taffie asked.

"I brought my clothes in a plastic bag," old Hansie said. "I'll dress here and the taxi will pick me up in front of the factory. It's almost two o'clock."

The newspaper sellers from Heidedal and Opkoms went noisily towards the streets, and the youngsters from the Children's Home climbed into the bus that had come to fetch them. It was the strangest feeling: suddenly Adam was the only one who had no plans for the long Saturday afternoon.

"Did you come on your bike?" Taffie asked as he unlocked his own bicycle.

"I couldn't," said Adam.

"Then you'll have to sit on my handlebars," said Taffie casually. "I'll pedal; you look out for the cars. Come on — I want to slip into the yard while my father is sleeping."

I'll probably break my neck today, Adam thought in a panic as he tried to keep his balance on the handlebars. I'm too dizzy to stay upright. But Taffie wasn't worried — his two hard, tanned hands gripped the handlebars firmly, and his sinewy arms were like steel cables on either side of Adam's hips.

108

"Do you and old Hansie . . . live close to each other?" Adam asked. "Careful — there's a motorbike coming."

"He boards in our backyard," said Taffie. "In an outside room. He's got no one — I don't know where his family are."

Taffie was almost in the middle of the road. Adam wanted to tell him to be careful, but his tongue felt too thick to lift.

"I'll take the shortcut past the station," Taffie said. "Andries Pretorius Street is always full of speed cops."

They shot around the corner over the underpass behind the station. Taffie was tough — his knees pumped up and down like steel pistons. "You know Long Street, don't you?" he asked. "We live near that piece of empty ground where they knocked down all the houses."

Long Street was a sad street: it seemed as though the soot from the trains had killed everything in sight. Here and there, some of the Saturday morning's wash was still on the line. If the washing hadn't been there, you might have thought that the people were dead too. At the top end of the street, many of the houses were empty; cats prowled the empty plots, moving among pieces of concrete and heaps of broken bricks.

"Why are they knocking everything down?" Adam asked, as they passed another empty plot.

"Who wants to live here?" Taffie asked and spat past Adam's right shoulder. "Everything dies here. My ma tried to plant flowers once, and when she watered them, the water lay on top of the soot. Didn't even reach the soil."

Lower down in the street, things improved, because there were fewer railway tracks. Here, there were gardens in front of the houses again: small bits of lawn, lemon trees, winter daisies. But Taffie didn't turn into any of the houses with gardens. He kicked open a gate and shot into a bare, sunbaked yard surrounded by a dilapidated wire fence.

"Shhhhh," he said urgently. He made a wide turn and stopped behind the outside room. "This is where Uncle Hansie lives."

Adam slipped off the handlebars and watched Taffie struggling with the key. Something was wrong with either the key or the lock because Taffie had to push and pull. But at the third try the door creaked open. Taffie went in first, then peered outside through a chink in the curtain. Adam heard him make a hissing noise and then Taffie's shoulders relaxed.

"Come on," said Taffie. "I don't think they saw us."

"Who?" said Adam nervously.

"My parents. Hang on, there's the box with the medicine."

He opened a box covered in greasy stains, and

scratched around among the bottles and tins. "You can't drink from the bottle," he said. "See if you can find a spoon somewhere."

Adam started searching, and the longer he searched, the more clearly he realized why old Hansie had to sell newspapers. The bed had no headboard; it stood angularly in the middle of the floor, covered with an old gray blanket full of burn marks, just like a bed in a prison cell. On the bed was a pair of socks which were full of holes, and a bottle-green jersey that had started to unravel. But on top of the old jersey was a big white card engraved with shiny black letters:

INVITATION
TO
COMMEMORATION SERVICE
FOR WAR VETERANS
SATURDAY, 15 JUNE
"See the conquering hero comes!
Sound the trumpets, beat the drums!"
THOMAS MORELL

Adam read Thomas Morell's words twice. Thomas Morell . . . who on earth was Thomas Morell? Was he also a war veteran? Whatever that might mean . . .

"Have you found one?" Taffie asked behind him.

Adam jumped, then went on looking for a spoon. There was a plate covered with breadcrumbs on the bare wooden table, an empty coffee mug covered in ants next to it. On the floor stood a pair of black shoes with bashed-in toes and frayed laces. There were a few books on the table. Adam bent down to read the titles: *Let's Play Chess, The Bible*, and a pile of photo stories with nurses on the cover. One of the books was losing its cover: *Bring Your Troubles*. Next to it was a little book with curled-up pages: *You and Your Arthritis*.

The more he looked, the more he saw. Hanging above the books was an old photograph in a warped frame: a dark-eyed woman with a boy on her lap. But the boy must have turned his head when the photo was taken, because his face was blurred, as though the woman were holding a small ghost — as though he'd never been really alive.

"There you are!" said Taffie suddenly. "Look, there — that's a spoon under the bed."

Adam bent down to pick up the spoon, but when he put his hand under the bed, something hissed. He went ice-cold and his head suddenly cleared.

"There's a snake or something under the bed," he stammered.

But Taffie laughed and lifted the blankets. "Look," he said. "It's only Lady."

"Lady?" Adam repeated, noticing something green in the dark under the bed. He nearly swallowed his tongue in fright but then, scared as he was, realized that it was a cat in a flat box: a mother cat with a row of kittens, their pink mouths against her stomach. The mother cat's eyes glowed like green lamps as she watched them.

"Miaaouw," the cat complained.

"It's only Lady," Taffie repeated, and wiped the spoon on his pants. "Here — drink two spoonfuls." He held out the medicine bottle and waited for Adam to swallow the sharp-tasting syrup.

Only when Adam had swallowed the syrup did he say: "Well, at least it *smelled* like cough mixture. It's kill or cure."

Taffie went back to the window and opened a chink in the curtains. "I'm off now," he said as he turned around. "There's an extra blanket on the chair. You can lie on that. I don't know if Uncle Hansie is coming to the room before the evening sales. But you'll wake up in time. Lock the door behind me and bring the key when you come to work. Or are you too ill to work tonight?"

"I must work," said Adam. "That's why I left Phameng." Something was bothering him. Both he and Taffie were whispering. Even when Lady's green eyes had made him jerk back in fright, Taffie had laughed soundlessly. It wasn't a real laugh; it sounded like a big dog panting.

And now Taffie was peering through the slit in the curtains as though he . . .

But it was silly. Only in Phameng was it like Sodom

and Gomorrah. This was an ordinary plot in the city. Taffie knew nothing of the rubbish dumps where the smoke never stopped billowing and you heard footsteps crunching behind you. He was only scared of his father—he'd said so, after all.

"Then I'll be off now," said Taffie, carefully turning the doorknob.

Suddenly Adam was scared. "Taffie—listen here. . . ."

"Get on with it," Taffie said. "I don't want them to catch me here."

"But . . ." Adam started stuttering, his throat closing with fright. "Taffie—are you sure I'm allowed to be here? Won't your parents—"

"Just forget about my parents," Taffie said and carefully turned the doorknob. "Just be dead quiet in here—"

"Yes, but . . ."

"I don't have time for all this talk, talk, talk," Taffie exclaimed.

"But you seem scared of something!" The words were out before Adam could stop them.

Taffie's lips twisted and his eyes were as hard as stone. "I'm not scared," he said abruptly. "It's just that I stay away from this house on a Saturday, that's all."

"But what about me?" asked Adam, in despair.

"Just don't let them see you going to work," Taffie

said. "As long as you stay here, they won't know about you. Besides — it's me who gets the chop on a Saturday. But forget about it — that's my worry."

He handed Adam the key. "Lock up when I've gone," he said. He slipped outside and suddenly Adam was alone in the semi-dark of old Hansie's room.

The cement floor was cold and the gray blanket thin, but Adam was so tired, and he had such a thick head, that he fell asleep almost immediately. I still wanted to peer through the chink in the curtains, he thought drowsily. I wanted to see if the back door of the house was still shut . . . if Taffie's parents . . . He tried to open his eyes. It's that medicine, he thought. It probably wasn't cough syrup — Taffie gave me the first thing he could lay his hands on.

He tried once more to lift his head, but his neck was too weak and it was impossible to keep his eyes open any longer. As they closed, he saw Lady's eyes blinking under the bed. He tried to think. Could cats blink their eyes? But it was too late. He was sleeping as though he'd been hit with a sandbag.

Lady didn't go away. In Adam's dream she crept out of the box, first one paw, then the next, her belly dragging on the cement floor. Her green eyes grew wild and she whipped her tail from side to side. "*Go away!*" he said to her in his dream, but she lay down in front of his face and lashed at his cheek with her paw.

115

"Got you," she said, so close to his face that he could smell her breath.

He couldn't believe it. She had pockmarks on her face like the boy at the rubbish dump. Ash clung to her ears; she pulled them back and bared her small front teeth.

"Go away!" he shouted and hit out at her, but she evaded him neatly. Her front paws moved as though he were a newly caught dove that she was playfully tossing into the air. He grew smaller; he could feel himself getting smaller. The bones in his body cracked and his head sang as everything shrank. The cat was as large as a lion. Her tail thudded on the floor.

"It's no use trying to get away," she growled. "I've got you."

"I'll give you something else," he shouted. "Please, I'll give you something else — I must go and look after my mother and my small brothers!"

"What can you give?" she asked, deep in her throat. "Tell me quickly!"

"A bantam cock," he stammered. "He's very clever . . . he's my aunt's. You can have him."

"Bantam chickens are just a handful of feathers," said Lady. "No meat. Don't try to fool me, d'you hear?"

"I'm sorry," he whispered. "I'll fetch . . . sparrows. There's a sparrow's nest on Dr. Marx's farm. It's easy to take them out. They're tame."

116

She lashed at him angrily with her nails. "Sparrows are only guts and feet," she hissed. "Are you stupid?"

At his wits' end, he rolled around on the cement floor, which was as hard as a rock. He knew it was only a dream, but he couldn't escape from it and kept on pleading.

"I don't have anything else!"

"Bring me a decent bird," Lady growled. "Go on, a big one! I must be able to toss it and pummel it; it must flap and fly and fall and struggle to fly again. That's what I'm looking for."

He tried to think, but the cold knifed into his legs and his heart beat in his throat. His mind refused to work. A bird that flapped and . . . fell . . . and struggled up again . . . And, suddenly, he remembered. That's what the piece of newspaper did against the windshield of the car, the day the wind caught old Hansie's newspapers. The paper bird had had big, square wings — and, big as it was, it had lived and shivered and shaken.

"I . . ." He didn't know how to explain it. "I can give you . . . a paper bird. I sell newspapers — I can easily get you one."

She stopped thudding her tail; her eyes became slits.

"Do you think I'm a fool?" she asked very slowly. "That's a worthless bird!"

"That's not true," he argued. "It's worth . . . it's worth a great deal!"

"Well, what is it worth? You're lying to me!"

"I'm speaking the truth," he whispered. "Why would I lie?"

"Then tell me what the paper bird is worth!"

"If I give it to you . . ." he started, struggling to collect his thoughts because his body was aching with cold. "If I give it to you . . . I'll have nothing left. I must sell newspapers, otherwise we won't have food and clothing."

"You're lying again," said Lady and swished her tail. "If you give me that bird, you'll still be able to get food and clothing. You'll just have to do something else."

"Like what?" he asked. "It's the only thing we have, Lady."

She licked her paw—her tongue was rough and pink. "You hate that bird," she said. "I know you hate it. You swore at it. You swore at it that day it flew into the car. Now you want to give me something you swore at."

"I only s . . . swear sometimes," he begged. "When I'm feeling down. Everyone feels down sometimes. It's true that the newspapers make me feel like that sometimes. But it's all I've got—I must keep on thinking that things will be better one day."

"They won't," she said maliciously.

"They will!" he shouted, and to his surprise she drew back. He looked again and she really was

118

retreating. "They will!" he shouted again. She shrank a little, disliking the noise he was making.

"And I won't give you . . . the paper bird, the bird with ink for blood!" he kept on shouting. "If you take it, everything will get worse. The bird belongs to me, d'you hear? I've sworn at it and wished it would die, but it belongs to me."

"Then I hope you get it to fly one day," she hissed spitefully through her teeth.

"And I will, too," he yelled and threw old Hansie's coffee mug at her.

As the mug clattered against the leg of the bed, he woke with a start and saw that it was getting dark in old Hansie's room. His face was on fire, even though his cheek was resting on the cold floor. Something was wrong with his chest; when he coughed, his whole body hurt. He sat up and saw the alarm clock next to old Hansie's books. The illuminated numbers of the clock showed it was six-fifteen. Time to go to the newspaper; the night sales were about to start.

Adam looked under the bed. Lady was watching him, her eyes narrowed to slits.

He got unsteadily to his feet and folded the gray blanket. His head felt as though it were burning. I dreamed something, he thought, and tried to remember the dream. Bit by bit it came back to him, as though he were flipping through an old schoolbook.

He couldn't remember it all. What fluttered vaguely through his mind was that he'd said the paper bird belonged to him, even though he'd cursed it so often. And that he would one day get it to fly.

And that felt very real to Adam, even though he knew it had only been a dream.

chapter 9

Taffie had made a fire even though it wasn't yet half-past ten. He had found a tomato box next to the trashcans of the apartment across the street to burn, and old Hansie had contributed a large piece of cardboard. Willem Maerman stood whistling while Taffie made the fire; he was used to having his underlings work for him.

Adam stood watching, without moving. He had coughed himself to a standstill, and his throat was burning as though he'd swallowed methylated spirits. "Stand close to the heat," he heard Willem say. "We don't want a dead body on our hands tonight."

"There's nothing about Phameng," said Taffie, looking through the newspaper again. "Wait a bit, here's something—it's about a house that was set on fire."

"Whose house?" Adam asked, his legs turning to water. "Whose house, Taffie?" It couldn't be . . . Modimo . . . please don't let it be Mama Dora's house! If the big boy with the marks on his face . . .

"Some guy's," said Taffie. "An official some-where." He folded the newspaper and looked up at the sky. "I swear we're going to be soaked tonight. I wish the movies would finish."

It's not Mama Dora's house, after all, Adam realized, his thoughts slow and uneasy. Modimo! Don't let them see Mama Dora's house! Just give me a chance with the newspaper money . . .

The cars started coming and he had to run with the newspapers. He counted out change, feeling relieved every time he managed to get it right. He ran from car to car while the light was red. He felt the warmth of the exhaust fumes against his legs, and he could have sworn that everyone could feel, from a distance, how hot his face was.

"You're lasting well," said old Hansie as they stood together under the white light of the street lamp. "I thought you were going to keel over."

"I feel like a primus stove," said Adam. "I stink of paraffin."

But the drivers were honking, and he had to run with the bundle of newspapers. He smelled printer's ink and the coming rain, he smelled his own hot primus smell, and he could still taste old Hansie's medicine in his mouth.

When the clock struck midnight, they finished. Adam was so tired and felt so ill that he rested his head against the cold window of the minibus, not caring about the shaking and the banging. Old Hansie sat opposite him, his face a gray smudge that only came into focus when they passed under the street lamps.

The safety jacket was pressing against his chin; he didn't have the strength to push it away. Halfway back, the few newspapers he still had left dropped from his hand — his fingers could no longer grip them properly. He jerked upright with fright, the cold running through his body in waves. He groped on the floor for the newspapers, feeling as though he were dying.

Suddenly, old Hansie touched his knee. "Sit up, boy. You really are ill. Remember, you're sleeping in my room again tonight."

Adam was too tired to speak; he simply nodded in the dark.

"Uncle Hansie, you looked very sharp when you came to work today. You looked like a new coin," said one of the boys from the Children's Home. "Was it nice, the party, this afternoon?"

"Lovely, lovely," said old Hansie, but his voice sounded sad. "Aaah . . . here we are. I only hope old Labuschagne doesn't give us a hard time with the cleaning tonight. Little Adam is going to drop in his tracks any moment now."

But it wasn't too long before they were able to leave. They had to walk the whole way, because old Hansie didn't have transport. Taffie pushed his bike and spoke very little. It felt as though there was no end to Long

Street—just when Adam thought Taffie's house was nearby, another empty plot appeared in the moonlight.

"There's still a light burning in your house," old Hansie said suddenly. "Taffie . . . ?"

"Yes—I see," Taffie said brusquely. "I swear I'm going to run away. I wonder what they'd do if I just disappeared one day."

They opened the sagging gate and Taffie motioned to Adam to be quiet. "See you tomorrow, Uncle Hansie," he said when they got close to the house. "Knock on my window if I oversleep again. Drat, I hate getting up early on Sunday mornings!"

"Sleep well," said old Hansie, and he watched Taffie open the back door of the house and walk into the square of light. "Come on, Adam boy, you must get comfortable. And I must give you some more medicine."

Old Hansie's room felt almost warm after the cold wind. Lady emerged from under the bed, a kitten hanging from her mouth, its paws limp.

"No, you're not bringing them into my bed," said old Hansie, and laughed. "You just stay in the box, Lady!" He switched on the kettle and scratched among his belongings. "I think coffee will be good for you, Adam, my boy. First the medicine and then hot coffee. That's what I always drink when I have flu."

"Thank you," said Adam, standing there in a daze as he listened to kind old Hansie speaking to him. He watched as the old man carefully put down the gray blanket for him on the floor.

Old Hansie sat on his bed and eased the tight shoes off his feet. He hung his best jacket on a wire hanger against the wall before he spooned instant coffee into the mugs.

"There's no milk," old Hansie said. "I always drink mine just like this — black. But I have sugar. Shall I give you some?"

"Just a little," Adam said. His throat felt thick; he could swear it wasn't just the flu. He swallowed the medicine, drank the coffee, and slowly his freezing body warmed. When he rolled over on his side to go to sleep, he saw old Hansie washing the mugs in a small bowl of water and slowly, as though the night had aged him, taking the Bible and sitting down on the edge of the bed to read it.

Adam's thoughts whirled. I'm too sick to pray, Modimo. I just want to sleep, Modimo.

But he didn't sleep because there was a sudden hullabaloo at the back door of Taffie's house. A woman could be heard protesting drunkenly, and then a door banged, making old Hansie's window rattle. There was a crash, and somewhere a second door banged. Moments later they heard an urgent knock at the door of the outside room.

"Coming," called old Hansie calmly. "Is that you, Taffie?"

Adam sat up. His heart felt as though it would jump out of its cage. Was there going to be trouble here as well? he thought wildly. They were everywhere, the troublemakers of Sodom and Gomorrah—pulling at the doors, they yelled everywhere . . .

Taffie tumbled into the room, his hair tousled and his face covered with dirty marks.

He'd been crying, Adam could see. He could hardly believe it. Taffie never cried.

"I'm sorry," he heard Taffie saying. "It's . . . it's a . . . they're all drunk, Uncle Hansie . . . and everybody's fighting. They're all . . . there again: the van der Nests, Dolf . . . the lot. My mother . . . she's as drunk as the men . . . I swear they're going to kill her tonight."

"I'll put down the bedcover for you," old Hansie said softly. "It's wide enough. You can cover yourself with one half. It's cold tonight."

Taffie sniffed loudly and moved the tin bath to one side, pushing old Hansie's dirty clothes into the corner.

It was quiet in the room for a long time, until Taffie suddenly burst out: "Why did they have me, if this is what they do? Why, Uncle Hansie? Why did they want me?"

Adam tried to hear old Hansie's reply, but all he heard was a vague mutter—he couldn't keep his eyes open any longer. He smelled his own primus smell, and a smoke-and-liquor smell that clung to Taffie's clothes, and he heard old Hansie moving slowly about the room, locking the door for the rest of the night. Then he dozed off.

At about three in the morning, Adam's body felt as if it was burning: his throat, his body, his skin. When he woke up, he was moaning involuntarily.

"What's the matter?" he heard old Hansie asking. "Adam, is it you making that noise, my boy?"

Adam couldn't help it; he kept on whimpering, unable to stop.

"Stupid light," he heard old Hansie say. "Stone dead again. Wait, I'll light the candle. What's wrong with you, Adam, my boy?"

The yellow circle of light came closer. Beyond the light, old Hansie's face was a dull, cracked smudge. "Are you ill, Adam?" old Hansie asked. "Adam?"

Taffie's head appeared in the candlelight. His hair was wild and his eyes were sleepy. "Perhaps you should give him medicine again, Uncle Hansie," Adam heard him say.

"Put three of those white pills in a little water," said old Hansie. "This fever's so bad it's going to give him a fit. Thanks, Taffie."

They pressed something cold against Adam's lips and he swallowed the sour stuff, but he wanted to cry, because it felt as though he were drifting away to a place where he would die.

"What's the matter, Adam?" he heard old Hansie asking and felt the man's hand on his body. "You'll soon feel better, my boy. Be quiet now — I won't leave you. You can lie down, Taffie. I'll stay with him until he's asleep."

"I'm scared," Adam heard himself saying. His body shook and he grabbed at the air — it had felt as though he were falling into a ditch.

"Scared of what?" asked old Hansie. "You can tell me, Adam."

"Of . . . this sickness," Adam muttered. He knew that he was speaking incoherently, but he couldn't stop himself. "And of staying in Phameng . . . the Casspirs . . . the people along the road . . . and the . . . if the people necklace Lady . . . and Mama Dora must go to work and she can't."

He knew there was something wrong with what he was saying, but his thoughts were like smoke being blown along by the wind. "The dog . . . at the stairs . . . and the people at school . . . I don't want to sleep under the stairs. I've got to get away. The big boy . . . he's watching me. I don't want to sleep under the stairs!"

"You're not going to," he heard old Hansie say. "You're sleeping in old Hansie's room, Adam, my boy."

"I'm scared," Adam whispered.

"I know," said old Hansie. "We're all scared, Adam. That's why Taffie is lying here; because he's scared of what's happening in his house. I'm scared, too . . . of the long nights . . . of getting old and dying. We're all scared. But we're not alone, Adam. The Lord is still there."

"He isn't here," said Adam. He felt dizzy.

"He is," said old Hansie. "He hasn't forgotten us, Adam. He knows about Taffie and you and about the . . . the necklaces . . . and about me. Tomorrow you'll get up and know that he was here when you were afraid."

Old Hansie sat with him for a long time. A few times Adam felt old Hansie's hand wiping his face with a wet cloth. The candle burned lower. The wind was rising: you could hear the fine sand in the backyard being blown against old Hansie's door.

Adam fell asleep while old Hansie sat beside him, his hand on Adam's body. It wasn't Modimo who was with him, he thought in confusion. It was old Hansie who was sitting up all night. The primus smell had gone. Old Hansie had taken it away.

But toward dawn he heard the bed creaking and he knew that old Hansie had gone to bed. Then Modimo must be here too, he thought. I'm not so scared anymore. It's pitch dark in the room, but I'm not so scared anymore.

As soon as it was light, old Hansie opened the curtains. Adam saw him waking Taffie and then slowly buttoning his shirt as he sat on the edge of the bed. The kettle sang when the water boiled, and the mugs tinkled as old Hansie lifted them out of the bowl.

"We'll give him a mug of coffee, too," he heard old Hansie say. "It'll do his fever good."

"I must get up," said Adam. But when he raised himself, his head spun. "What's the time, Taffie?"

"Almost half-past six," said Taffie, rubbing the sleep from his eyes.

"You're staying right here," old Hansie said suddenly. "See here, Adam, you're heaps better than last night, but this thing isn't going to get cured overnight. We'll be okay with the newspapers — you stay right here."

"I can't," said Adam. "You don't understand. I came . . . to help my mother buy clothes and things. It's because my mother had the twins that I had to come and work this weekend."

"You stay right here," repeated old Hansie as if he hadn't heard Adam. He measured the coffee powder into the mugs with a teaspoon and gestured toward the bed. "Taffie, get us some rusks from the tin down there. It's the square tin next to Lady's box. My stomach is hollow this morning."

"Mine, too," said Taffie as he dragged out the tin. "I haven't eaten since yesterday morning."

Adam watched Taffie opening the tin containing a few rusks and putting it down in front of them on the blanket. Old Hansie handed them each a mug of black coffee, and Taffie hungrily dunked the rusks and stuffed them into his mouth.

"Give Adam some, too," said old Hansie, his dull eyes looking at Adam.

"Help yourself," said Taffie, his mouth full.

The rusks tasted good. Adam hadn't realized how hungry he really was. He must still be ill. He thought, because his thinking remained confused. If a rusk was like an asparagus, he thought, swallowing a big piece, it could start growing while I'm eating the front part. If rusks were like asparagus, I could eat and eat without having to reach for the tin.

"Have some more," said old Hansie, cradling the mug of hot coffee in his hands. He wrinkled his nose to push up his glasses and angled his head to find a clear piece of lens through which to look at Taffie. "You said Dolf was there last night, too? I thought you said the Welfare was going to take him away if he started drinking again."

"Not that Dolf, Uncle Hansie," Taffie said and got up to pour more hot water into his mug. "If only it had been Uncle Dolf Windbag! It was our Dolf — my brother Dolf. It was him who bashed me up like this."

"Did you say something to annoy him?" old Hansie asked.

"I'd hardly opened my mouth," said Taffie and his lips tightened. "Last time he promised he'd stop drinking. But when I reminded him of that last night, he grabbed a bottle . . . I thought he was going to kill me." He pulled a frayed end off the worn blanket, his face as hard as stone. "I'll never call him my brother again. He's no more my brother than . . . than that stupid cat!"

"You can't say that," old Hansie said slowly. "Dolf's not a bad guy. It's the drink. . . ."

"There's no way that he's my brother," said Taffie. "I'd sooner say . . . you were my brothers!"

Old Hansie got up slowly and put the lid on the coffee tin. "Have more rusks," he said. "Go on, Adam, have some. Tomorrow we'll buy more."

When Adam tried to get up, they made him lie down once more. "Won't somebody come and look in here?" he asked before they left. "If someone finds me here, it'll be . . ."

Taffie gave a strange laugh. Then he said: "Today no one will move in that house. They'll lie where they dropped."

After old Hansie and Taffie had left, Adam just lay there. He was feeling lightheaded from the medicine, but his heart was as heavy as a sack of coal. Now, nothing means anything anymore, he thought, and his head hurt as he frowned. It was no use my coming to town and sleeping under the stairs . . . I don't have the money to take home. My money won't be nearly as much as I usually take home at weekends.

Birds were walking about on old Hansie's flat roof.

Adam could hear their hard claws scraping against the corrugated iron. They're doves, he thought sleepily. They're cooing right above my head. The noise bothered him, and he couldn't think straight. When he tried to think about the money, the cooing of the doves interfered with his thoughts.

Stretching, Lady emerged from under the bed and sat listening to the doves, her head cocked. Her tail swished gently — it seemed as though she were tired of her children and wanted company. Adam heard the faint mewing of the kittens.

In the daylight, Lady's eyes were yellow — almost as bright as if a candle were burning inside her head. Adam stared at the yellow light. Her eyes were like two windows through which light fell. Green at night, yellow by day. Magdalene, he thought, would like to have a cat. She would be able to make up stories about a cat's eyes . . . about the light burning inside a cat's head.

It tired him to lie looking at the cat's eyes; he was so tired he just wanted to sleep. But when Lady came closer, he knew that on no account did he want to dream again.

He must have slept again, because he woke, cold with fear, when old Hansie and Taffie rattled the door. It was just after one. I'm almost well, he thought as he sat up. I slept like the dead.

"Stupid lock," he heard old Hansie say, and the door creaked as it opened. They looked windblown — only a few strands of hair lay across old Hansie's bald patch.

"Boy, did we work!" said Taffie, who had a piece of dried sausage in his hand which he was chewing busily. "There was a scoop in the morning paper: something about a guy who shot four people at a disco."

"Nothing about Phameng?" asked Adam. Just saying the name made him feel alarmed again. Phameng was still there, the fires smoldering between the houses, Ma waiting for him to come back.

"I didn't look," said Taffie. "But it's probably just the same . . . it's been going on forever." Deftly, he emptied his pocket and dropped something in front of Adam. "That's yours."

"My what?" Adam asked and picked up the heavy paper packet from the blanket.

"Your newspaper money," said Taffie and bit off a large piece of dried sausage. "Uncle Hansie and I sold your newspapers as well. Willem Maerman nearly had a fit because we lied to him. We said you were waiting at the corner and when the bus dropped us, you weren't there, of course, but by then it was too late to get one of the kids from the Children's Home."

Adam gaped at Taffie. "But . . ." he began. "But then you should take the money!"

"We'll take it another time," said old Hansie, un-hooking Lady's claws from his trouser leg. "After all, it was we who said you must stay here — so we had to make sure there would be enough for you to take home to your mother and the babies. That's fair, isn't it?"

Adam sat with the packet of money in his hand. He couldn't speak. My head is still sick, he thought. I can't speak properly. He swallowed, and when he could get the words past the lump in his throat, they were in Sesotho: "*Ke a leboha . . . ke re, ke a leboha* — Thank you, I say. Thank you!"

It was impossible to add anything more. So, weak though he was, he rose, folded the blanket, and put it on the chair. "I must go now," he said, not knowing which way to look. "My mother will be waiting for me."

"Will you be okay?" Taffie asked, scratching his head. "Shouldn't you spend another night here? The newspapers said there was going to be trouble all weekend — suppose they pot you?"

"Pot?" asked Adam, disliking the sound of the word.

"Yes, man, pot . . . shoot! Suppose they shoot any-body who leaves his house?"

Adam's mouth was dry. "They . . . won't pot kids," he said, and added weakly, "I don't think they will."

He got up to leave. "My real problem is getting past the people waiting along the road. I'm scared they'll burn down my aunt's house."

"It won't happen," said old Hansie, but his voice was uncertain. "You must tell me if you want to spend another night here, Adam, my boy. I don't mind."

"My mother will be waiting for me," Adam repeated.

"You didn't have anything with you, did you?" Taffie asked at the door.

"Only the wheel, and I left that somewhere."

He looked back. The room was small and dark, and it smelled of cat and coffee and dried sausage and people. He smelled the medicine old Hansie had given him, and the warm, woolly smell of the blanket he'd slept under. He knew it was silly, but he wished he could turn back, that he could stay in the room.

It isn't just the blanket or the coffee, he thought. It's the people. I'm scared of leaving. I'm also scared of the road and of Phameng. There are many voices calling me. Far away, in Phameng, the cries of Ma's two babies were calling — behind him the room was calling. Or perhaps it wasn't the room. Perhaps it just felt like that because he and Taffie and old Hansie had been brothers for a while.

"Don't let them bash you," said Taffie.

"Come back if you have to," said old Hansie, looking like an old, battered rooster.

"*Salang hantle* — stay well," Adam said to them. And then softly to old Hansie: "*Sala hantle, Ntatemoholo!*" He'd done it — he'd called old Hansie Grandpa.

As Adam still felt lightheaded after the fever, it seemed a long way to Phameng. And since he had to check the buildings and the posts, and the trees at the side of the road as well, and constantly heard noises behind him, and saw frightening shadows near the road, the walk home was endless.

Adam walked along the fence of Pelonomi Hospital, a cold, creeping sweat trickling down his body. Had the road always been this dirty? he wondered. Had there always been so many bits of paper blown against the fence, so many broken tires and so much rusted iron?

There were broad dust tracks on the black tar: big vehicles had passed this way.

I must go on, he thought. I've nowhere else to go. I can't go back to old Hansie's room. If I want to be *monna* — a man — I must go home today.

He saw the Casspirs from a long way away. They were parked where the dirt road turned off the tarred road. His heart thudded; there were men in uniforms in the veld next to the Casspirs. But something had changed: they were standing quietly, and one had his hands gripped behind his head and was swinging his torso from side to side as though doing exercises, as though relaxing his tired body. They didn't grab their guns. They didn't speak over the bullhorn. They simply watched him pass in silence.

Who scares me most? Adam wondered. The people with the Casspirs, or the people along the road? He swallowed and started running, fear chasing him. He saw cattle; they looked like small Casspirs rising in front of him. The wind blew over the rubbish dump and the ash whirled into the air.

Then he saw there was something wrong with the hotel. Part of the roof was missing and where it had been there was a gaping black hole, as if a large burning object had dropped from the sky and smashed through it. Farther down the street, one of the tall poles had snapped, its back broken.

What if Mama Dora's house has gone . . . if I get there and there's only a black hole?

He smelled smoke. Water must have been poured on the fires, because the smell was that of fire doused with water. The streets were quiet. The tin bath in which the children always played lay on its side against one of the fences. But the children were not there; they had probably been called inside.

Looking around, he could see that the fire had been everywhere: charred cardboard and planks from vegetable crates lay in the street. Every time the wind gusted, crumbling half-burnt papers were blown into the air.

If the burnt paper keeps on crumbling, Adam thought, the whole world will be filled with ash and soot. The wind carries everything farther — once paper is burnt, it blows all over the earth.

He ran past the fence on which, during the night, someone had painted FREEDOM IS HEAVEN. He saw diapers flapping in the backyards. Adam fingered the money in his pocket. I wonder what their faces will look like when I open the door?

In front of the small brick church of the Assemblies, Adam halted. ASSEM was all that remained on the wall . . . the rest of the word had gone! It must have disappeared in the blackness of the fire. The wooden cross had gone; the statue of the Good Shepherd had been pulled from its niche. Where the stained-glass window had been there was nothing but a hole, grimy with soot.

He felt fright numbing his limbs.

Modimo! Modimo! The Shepherd couldn't be gone! His mind was a jumble of thoughts. He was too shaken to feel ill any longer. The Shepherd couldn't be gone. Modimo! He was angry, too, because some human being had destroyed the rainbow window and the Shepherd and the wooden cross with fire.

We'll make a new wooden cross! he wanted to yell. We'll put in new windows. We'll scrub these walls. We . . . we . . .

If Ntate had been here, he would have said that people don't behave like this. People treat each other with respect, Ntate always said. Modimo is a God of love, not of people who want to kill and knife each other.

Adam looked back. The quietness of the streets made him more frightened than ever. Perhaps the people were all dead . . . He started running, his breath whistling in his throat. He clutched the packet of money, almost too scared to look.

Mama Dora's house was still there; it was still standing! From a distance he saw the bantam rooster sitting on the fence. In the yard, the borrowed baby clothes fluttered on the washing line.

He pushed open the door and his jaw dropped. There sat Samuel, right in front of him, with Edward and Magdalene and Maria. They looked up when he came in. Samuel was the first to speak.

"You've . . . you've come back!" he said, smiling broadly.

Adam could barely speak. "But what are you doing here? Aren't you supposed to stay at home?"

Samuel looked embarrassed. "I had to pass here to fetch something. And I just wanted to find out . . . if . . . if you'd come back."

Behind them Edward was shouting, "Adam's back! Ma, come quickly! Adam's back!"

Adam heard the bed creaking. Then the bedroom door opened. Ma had been lying down; sleep had creased her cheek, and her headcloth was askew. Behind her, Evon started crying. Adam heard Mama Dora

140

saying, "Shhhh . . . shhhh . . . your brothers will wake up. . . ."

He watched Ma without moving, clenching his teeth to stop them chattering. It was as though real fear had only just hit him, as though he'd been running all the time and only just realized what might have happened to him.

It smells just like old Hansie's room here, he wanted to say. It's all the same; old Hansie's room and Mama Dora's house. . . . It smelled of blankets and warmth . . . and people.

Softly he let out his breath, and for the first time the tightness in his chest eased.

"You've come back!" said Ma, her face shining as she looked at him. "I couldn't sleep because of you — when there was all that shooting in the streets, I thought you would never come back."

"Did they shoot, Ma?" he asked. "Were there fires nearby?"

"Lots," she said. "But are you all right, Adam? Weren't you hurt?"

"I was sick, Ma," he said. "My chest was burning and I had a dreadful cough. But my friends at the newspaper looked after me."

He took the packet of money out of his pocket and put it down in front of her. "This is for the clothes and the diapers," he said. "I didn't buy anything — not even polony."

Samuel stood up. His and Edward's arms hung at

their sides as though they didn't have the strength to move them.

"I bet you were scared," said Samuel.

Then it was Edward who spoke, quickly and in a high voice, as he had that time when he'd been the first to spot the swarm of grasshoppers coming. "My brother knows what he's doing," said Edward. "He's not afraid of anything. We don't have a father anymore, that's why Adam is *monna* now."

To Adam, it felt like a dream: nothing had changed here. The cloth on the table was covered with crumbs after the meal; Moses's shirt was hanging over the back of the chair because he was probably out in the cold without one. Evon whimpered in the bedroom, and over everything hung the smell of babies.

But he was back, he was back! The hurt and fright at the sight of the burned, blackened church still filled his breast, and he still trembled when he thought about the road he had traveled.

Perhaps it was because he was ill; perhaps it was because he'd seen it all and had managed to pass the Casspirs and the rubbish dumps that he felt older — older than Samuel, and almost older than Ma, too.

"It was terrible here, Adam," said Samuel.

"I've seen it all," he said. "The church, too. Everything is black — as though we're living in hell." As he spoke, he felt cold again.

"We still have each other," said Ma quietly.

Adam thought about Lady and th
been given by old Hansie, the candle,
to the tin of rusks. "And there are still
he said and frowned, because that was
and he was too tired to explain.

"We prayed without closing our eyes,
said suddenly. "With the bread in our mouths."

"I know," he said. "That's probably why there was
no one along the road."

But Magdalene's face looked troubled, and her eyes
filled with tears. "Those people at the road stopped
Kgatwane from coming," she said, her lip trembling.
"There was nothing under the stone. Only a bug."

"Maybe Kgatwane sent you a bug," said Edward
and rolled his eyes.

Adam looked around; he was too lightheaded to think
straight. I'd forgotten about Kgatwane, he realized.
How could I remember everything?

"There's no silly lizard," said Maria, shaking her
head.

"There is," Adam heard himself saying. "But I told
you, he can only come when it's quiet. Perhaps . . .
perhaps we should send a bird to tell him that you're
still waiting for him, that it's quieter now, and that he
can come."

"What bird?" Magdalene asked, no longer pouting
as much, though there were still tears in her eyes.
"We don't have a bird."

"Then we'll make one," said Adam, and he fumbled for the piece of newspaper kept next to Mama Dora's stove for lighting the fire. "Look, Magdalene!" He started folding, his thoughts racing ahead. He folded and folded and made a bird with an angular body and two big wings.

"That's not a bird," said Magdalene.

"Of course it is," he said. "Smell his blood."

She pressed her nose into the folds of newspaper and looked at him with her big eyes. "I don't smell anything," she said reproachfully.

"If you smell properly, you can smell the ink. That's his blood," said Adam. "All the newspaper birds have black blood. It's ink blood."

"But he can't fly," Magdalene cried, sniffing hard.

"He can," said Adam. But Magdalene gave him a questioning look, and he opened the door to the backyard, where the chickens were scratching and clucking.

"Listen carefully, Magdalene," he said, and it felt as though he were back in his dream, right at the end. "If this bird flies when I throw it, you'll know: Kgatwane will hear that you're waiting for him. If the bird flies, you'll know that everything is going to get better."

"Will it?" Edward asked. "You can't be sure."

"I can," said Adam. "We must not lose hope. Nothing is completely bad. Not everybody . . . not everybody wants to burn and kill. There are lots of good people. Lots."

144

"Kgatwane is real," said Magdalene, and her voice trailed upward as if she were asking a question. Carefully she touched the wing of the paper bird and then sniffed her fingers as though she wanted to smell blood.

"Have you seen a paper bird fly?" she asked. "Really and truly fly?"

"If you work at the newspaper long enough," said Adam, "then, in the end, you will see that they can fly."

"But do they fly every, every day?" Magdalene insisted.

He folded the paper bird's head; the beak was nice and sharp.

"Hmm-hmm," he said slowly. "Some days they keep dropping down. Some days they're just plain stupid — then I hate them. But that's when I'm discouraged."

"Are you dis . . . what's it . . . dis . . . now?"

"How can I be discouraged now?" he asked. "When we're all together again! I brought the money . . . Kgatwane will come! The bird won't drop to the ground today."

Magdalene's little face was serious. "Let him fly," she said. "Kgatwane will come. Shall we pray for him to fly?"

Adam did not know what to say.

"I suppose we could pray," he said after a while.

"Then I'll pray first," Magdalene said, and shut her eyes tightly.

Adam went outside and she went with him, only stopping at Kgatwane's stone.

"It's this stone," she said, pointing. "Does Kgatwane know?"

"He knows everything," said Adam, and raised the beak of the newspaper bird. He could still smell the doused fires, but a brisk wind was blowing and the air was clearing. Somewhere, in one of the houses, an afternoon church service was being held. He could hear people singing. He threw the ink bird downwind and the paper wings trembled and then stiffened.

And as the bird glided over the roof, Adam could have sworn that it really was alive.

Glossary

auk	boy
ausi	girl, sister
Bona sekolo	Good school; the rest of the song's words (in the Sotho language) mean, Come to school; the bell is ringing. . . .
bos	bush
Casspirs	armored police vehicles used during unrest in the black townships
Dumela	a greeting (Good day!)
duwweltjies	small prickly thorns, commonly found in grass patches and along footpaths
lekker kos	good food
Modimo	the Lord, God
mosadi	woman
to necklace	a method of killing alleged police collaborators: a rubber tire is placed around the victim's neck, then set on fire
Ntate	Father
popi	doll
putu	mealie or corn porridge
shebeen	a kind of bar, run from a private house in a township, that sells alcoholic drinks after hours, often with no license
sjambok	a whip, traditionally made from rhinoceros hide
tche	no

tjaila	time off work, a chance to relax
veld	open area of grassland in a rural environment
vetkoek	a bread roll or scone, made of yeast and flour and fried in oil — somewhat similar to a doughnut

ABOUT THE AUTHOR

MARETHA MAARTENS is a popular and highly acclaimed author in her native South Africa. Her writing for young people has been praised for portraying the political situation in South Africa realistically, with warmth and understanding of the human values involved. "When I notice another person—especially a child or young person—faced with an experience or problem he or she cannot assimilate, or I myself face a problem, I write about it in an attempt to make sense of it," she says.

She is married to Dr. Hennie Maartens, a minister in the Dutch Reformed Church. They have two daughters and live in Bloemfontein, South Africa.